Elizabeth stepped into the room, glancing in confusion from Tia to Conner. "Megan told me you were here." She focused on Conner's sweatpants, then glanced back up at his face. "Conner? What's going on?"

"What do you mean?" he asked, running a hand through his hair. "Tee and I were just hanging out."

Elizabeth glanced down at her black leather sandals and nodded. "Then why are you acting so weird?" she asked in a quiet voice.

Maybe because you couldn't have picked a worse moment to barge in here, Conner thought. But he just shrugged. "We weren't expecting you."

"Oh," Elizabeth said, still not sounding completely convinced. She stared at Conner. "I guess I just thought that *we* were going to hang out tonight."

Conner sighed. What was her deal? "We were. And then you had to work late. Remember?"

Elizabeth's cheeks flushed pink, and she shook her head. Finally her face relaxed. "God, I'm sorry," she told them. "I don't know what's wrong with me. Of course you guys were just hanging out."

"Right," Conner said. He could feel Tia's gaze on him. He had to get out of the intensity of this room. Now.

Don't miss any of the books in SWEET VALLEY HIGH
SENIOR YEAR, an exciting series from Bantam Books!

Visit the Official Sweet Valley Web Site on the Internet at:

http://www.sweetvalley.com

Francine Pascal's SVH senioryear

Three Girls and a Guy

CREATED BY
FRANCINE PASCAL

BANTAM BOOKS
NEW YORK · TORONTO · LONDON · SYDNEY · AUCKLAND

RL: 6, AGES 012 AND UP

THREE GIRLS AND A GUY
A Bantam Book / April 2000

Sweet Valley High® is a registered trademark of Francine Pascal.
Conceived by Francine Pascal.
Cover photography by Michael Segal.

Produced by 17th Street Productions, Inc.
33 West 17th Street
New York, NY 10011.

ISBN: 0-553-49315-9

Visit us on the Web! www.randomhouse.com/teens

Published simultaneously in the United States and Canada

*Bantam Books is an imprint of Random House Children's Books, a
division of Random House, Inc. BANTAM BOOKS and the rooster
colophon are registered trademarks of Random House, Inc. Bantam Books,
1540 Broadway, New York, New York 10036.*

PRINTED IN THE UNITED STATES OF AMERICA

OPM   0 9 8 7 6 5 4 3 2 1

To Shannon Walsh

Andy Marsden

I never thought relationships could really be that hard. I mean, what's the big deal? You meet someone you like, and you hang out. Have fun together. What's so difficult about that?

Okay, yeah, I've listened to Tia and Maria and Conner and Liz moan and groan about the opposite sex on multiple occasions. But I always thought that they were just being melodramatic. Trying to create some excitement in their otherwise dull, predictable lives.

But ever since I've started seeing Six, I've learned otherwise.

So either I've developed a flair for the dramatic or relationships are <u>not</u> easy.

TIA RAMIREZ

I NEVER THOUGHT THAT MUCH ABOUT RELATIONSHIPS. SURE, I WAS IN ONE FOR THREE YEARS, BUT THAT SORT OF JUST HAPPENED. I LOVED ANGEL, AND WE WERE TOGETHER. PERIOD.

BUT NOW THAT ANGEL AND I ARE DONE, I REALIZE THAT I'M NOT REALLY A RELATIONSHIP TYPE OF GIRL. AT LEAST NOT ANYMORE. THINK ABOUT IT. I'M SEVENTEEN. I SHOULD BE A FREE SPIRIT—OUT THERE FLIRTING, DANCING, KISSING—UNATTACHED AND INDEPENDENT. BESIDES, I'M STILL NOT TOTALLY OVER ANGEL, SO IT WOULDN'T BE FAIR TO GET SOMEONE ELSE TANGLED UP IN MY CONFUSED PSYCHE.

THERE. IT'S DECIDED. I'M JUST HAVING FUN FOR THE REST OF THE YEAR. NO RELATIONSHIPS FOR ME.

. . . UNLESS, OF COURSE, I MEET SOMEONE ELSE AS COOL AS ANGEL.

Jessica Wakefield

I've been in so many relationships, I can't even count them. And they all have something striking in common: <u>None</u> of them have worked out. Yep, that's right. Nada. Zilch. Zero.

I always thought that I had to be in a relationship. Like I'd be nothing without a boyfriend. But now I see that that is <u>so</u> not the case. In fact, I think it would be good for me to learn how to function without constantly focusing on some guy in my life.

So I'm not only staying away from relationships — I'm staying away from guys in general. That's right. I'll be living in a boy-free zone.

Of course, if Evan <u>wanted</u> to kiss me, I wouldn't exactly push him away or anything.

I didn't say I was giving up on kissing.

Conner McDermott

I've never been in a relationship this long.

I should just bail. Run and never look back.

I would, you know. Except for one thing.

This is Liz.

Elizabeth Wakefield

After breaking up with Todd at the end of junior year, I swore that I wouldn't get into another relationship for a while. For so long my identity had been melded into Todd's. I wasn't just Liz. I was LizandTodd. ToddandLiz. And after things were over with him, I was more than ready to be on my own.

Then I met Conner.

But things are so different with Conner than they were with Todd. I'm with Conner because I love him, not because I'm expected to be. And Conner is not the type to want to be in a suffocating relationship. He needs his space. So even though I'm his girlfriend, I'm still Liz. Not LizandConner. ConnerandLiz.

And that's how I like it.

Uncomfortable Vibes

Ken Matthews woke up on Saturday morning in a seriously grumpy mood. Which was funny, considering that last night should have been one of the best nights of his life. *Should have been* were the operative words here, however. Although Ken did receive a special spirit award from the *Sweet Valley Tribune*, his father had neglected to show up for the big moment. And that had put more than a slight damper on the evening.

I can't believe he bailed out on me for some woman, Ken thought, throwing off his plaid comforter and grabbing his gray SVH-football sweatpants from the shag-carpeted floor. Sure, Ken understood that his father needed to date. But did that have to mean that Ken was now delegated to the very bottom of his father's priority list—somewhere below going to the dentist and cleaning out the garage?

Ken sighed. Normally he didn't tell his father when things were bothering him. It seemed too hard and too pointless to have that type of a conversation

1

with the guy. But this time was going to be different. Ken wasn't going to let him off easy.

I guess I'll have to wait until this afternoon for that, he thought as he walked out of his room. Ken hadn't heard his father come home last night, so he figured that he must have slept at Asha's. *Man. I wouldn't be surprised if he moved in with her altogether and left me here alone.*

But as Ken headed down the staircase, he heard his father's voice, followed by a woman's laughter.

Ken stopped in place. Part of him wanted to run back up the stairs and stay in his room until she left.

But he wasn't a child, and he wasn't going to hide out in his own home.

Still, as he rounded the corner and walked into the kitchen, he sort of wished he had. It was just so . . . weird, seeing his father and this strange woman sitting and eating in his little breakfast nook, Asha looking perfectly at home in Ken's father's dark blue bathrobe, the *Sweet Valley Tribune* laid out before her on the square, black Formica table. And they were so busy drinking their coffee and eating their bagels that they didn't even notice Ken when he walked in. Ken's father reached out to massage Asha's slender shoulder.

"Uh, hey, guys," Ken mumbled.

Asha immediately broke away from Mr. Matthews, closing the bathrobe tighter around her body. "Morning," she said, pushing her red-framed glasses up on her face. A dark tendril of hair slipped out of the bun on top of her head, and a flush jumped to both of her cheeks. She forced a smile.

Ken's own cheeks felt like they were flaming up, which really annoyed him. She was the one who should be embarrassed, not him.

Ken's father was the only one who acted like nothing was out of the ordinary. He ran a hand through his thinning blond hair, gulped down his last drop of coffee, and said, "Morning, Ken."

Ken blinked. Was his dad even going to apologize for last night? Did he even remember?

"Would you like a bagel?" Asha asked, standing up. "Some coffee?"

Okay, this was completely screwed up. She was acting like she lived here now.

"No," Ken said, walking over to the refrigerator. "Thanks." He pulled out the orange juice, then shot another glance at his father. Nothing.

Ken put the juice container down on the counter. He couldn't take this anymore. "Dad?" he began. "Did you just completely forget about last night or what?"

Mr. Matthews looked up from the paper. His blue eyes opened wide. "Last night?" Asha put down her own bagel midbite and watched Ken's father warily.

"You know, the awards dinner?" Ken reminded him, even though he was fairly certain his dad knew exactly what he was talking about. "You promised me you'd come. I looked all over for you like an idiot."

Ken's father put down the paper, leaning forward. "Now's not the time, Ken. Let's talk about this when we're alone."

Now's not the time to what? Apologize? Ken thought, fuming. He grabbed a glass out of the overhead cabinet and slammed it down on the counter, sloppily pouring some juice into it and almost causing the glass to overflow. "Yeah, whatever," he muttered, taking a sip.

"No, Ken, we're sorry," Asha suddenly put in, surprising both Ken and, by the looks of his expression, Ken's father.

Mr. Matthews placed a hand on Asha's wrist. "Asha, you don't have to—"

"No, no." She took off her glasses and regarded Ken with apologetic brown eyes. "We had these reservations at Le Bon Coin. A friend got them for us. They would've been a big deal to cancel."

Ken traced the rim of his glass with his finger, trying not to explode. What was with all this "we" crap? Fine, so they were going out, but since when did Asha become his father's official spokesperson? And since when was keeping a reservation at a trendy restaurant more important than showing up for your son's awards dinner? Ken deserved a *real* apology. From his father.

Ken glanced over at him now. His dad was folding the newspaper and standing up, as if everything had been neatly explained.

"You could have at least called to tell me that," Ken said.

4

Mr. Matthews's round cheeks tinged with pink. He rolled up the newspaper like a poster, wrapping both of his big hands around it. "Ken, Asha just apologized," he warned. "Watch your tone."

Yeah, Ken thought, *that's just the problem. Asha apologized. Not you.*

"No, Ken's right," Asha said, clearing the table. She carried the two black ceramic mugs and plates over to where Ken was standing, then put them in the sink. "We should've called. I don't know what we were thinking." She turned to Ken, placing one hand on her hip. "I'm really sorry. It won't happen again."

All Ken could do was stare down at his glass of orange juice. But he was thinking about his mom. And how she never would have let this happen in the first place.

"I'm just used to being alone," Asha continued as she turned on the water at the sink and began to rinse off the plates and mugs. "But I know that's gotta change if I'm going to be a part of your lives. I'm going to have to start considering *your* feelings as well as your father's."

Ken watched Asha silently as she opened the dishwasher and loaded it up. Who *was* this woman? And in what way did she think she was going to be a part of Ken's life?

Asha closed the dishwasher and looked at Ken, wiping her hands dry with a dishrag. "So. Apology accepted?"

Ken fidgeted with the edge of the counter. "Uh, yeah."

Asha smiled an enormous, toothy smile. Then she leaned against the counter, crossing her arms over her chest. "Hey, you know what I'd like to do?" she asked, glancing from Ken to his father.

Ken's father tapped the rolled-up newspaper against the table. "What?"

"Make dinner for you two guys on Monday night. I'm a killer cook, and that way Ken and I could get to know each other better."

At that moment Ken felt like he'd rather eat glass.

Ken's father walked over and kissed Asha's delicate cheek. His big, ex-football-player's body dwarfed Asha's narrow frame. "You really don't need to do that."

"I know," Asha responded, her eyes lighting up with amusement. "I don't *have* to do anything. But it would be fun."

Ken's father shrugged. "Okay. Whatever you want."

They both looked at Ken for his response. Ken was still pissed off, but what was the point of telling them? His opinion didn't seem to matter anyway.

"Sure," he told them. "Whatever."

Andy Marsden took a moment to collect himself in front of Six Hanson's front door on Saturday night. Letting out a deep breath, he pulled down on his green-and-blue-striped long-sleeved T-shirt, ran a hand through his red hair, and closed his eyes.

Don't be nervous, he told himself. *It's not like this*

is your first date. Besides, the girl's crazy about you.

Andy's eyes flew open. That was kind of the problem, wasn't it? That Six was so obviously into him when Andy still wasn't sure how he felt about her?

Relax, Andy told himself. *She's a great girl, she's beautiful, and you like hanging out with her. Tonight will be fun.*

Andy pulled down on his shirt one more time, then rang the Hansons' doorbell.

Travis, Six's brother, answered the door, and Andy felt an unexpected fresh wave of nervousness. *Chill,* Andy thought. *Talking to Travis will give you extra time to mellow out.*

On his so-called date the night before, talking to Travis had been the least nerve-racking part of the evening.

"Hey, man," Travis said, lifting his chin and slapping Andy's hand in greeting.

"Uh, hi. I mean . . . hey," Andy returned. His face heated up when he realized he sounded like a stuttering idiot. He had to get a grip. He didn't want Travis thinking he was a moron.

Travis was dressed in his usual outdoorsy, disheveled way—a pair of tan carpenter-style shorts hung loose on his skinny hips, his worn flannel shirt was misbuttoned, causing it to hang crookedly, and his blue-and-black Teva sandals looked like they just might fall apart at any minute. But the guy was so fit and so tan that he never actually *looked* sloppy, even though that was exactly how he dressed.

Maybe if I really get into this outdoors stuff, I'll be able to get away with that too. Then all the chicks will want me. Andy smiled, laughing inwardly at his own joke and relaxing somewhat. A gorgeous sophomore might be interested in him at the moment, but the days when droves of girls would be chasing him still seemed far off.

"Playing doorman again?" Andy asked.

"It's what I do. Come on in," Travis said, holding the door open. "Six'll probably be a while. She's into keeping the guy waiting and everything."

"Ah," Andy said. He stepped inside the house. "Gotcha." He glanced around as he followed Travis into the living room. Andy had only been in the Hansons' house once before, but he already liked it. It was exactly what he had expected—casual and lived-in looking, with its uncarpeted old wooden floors, plain but comfortable-looking furniture, and books, framed photographs, and random sports equipment pushed into every available space. Still, the place managed not to look messy. Just welcoming.

"You want anything to drink?" Travis asked, stretching his arms over his head.

"Nah. I'm all right, thanks," Andy responded.

Travis dropped down onto the brown corduroy couch in the center of the room. "Well, have a seat, then. Trust me, Six's going to take her time."

"Oh. Okay." Actually, Andy could deal with waiting. Maybe by the time Six made her grand entrance, Andy would be completely calm. *Yeah, right.* He sat down next to his impromptu host, wiping his clammy palms on his khakis.

"I was just doing some research for my back-packing route this summer," Travis explained, motioning to a bunch of books on the battered wooden coffee table before them. There was *Let's Go: Europe*, Lonely Planet's *Europe on a Shoestring*, and an open spiral notebook with all sorts of notes jotted down on it.

"Really? God, I am so jealous of you," Andy said. He picked up the *Let's Go* book and flipped through it. "Do you know which places you're gonna go?"

"Everywhere." Travis grinned, his blue eyes twinkling with enthusiasm. "Seriously. I mean, as long as I really rough it, I can afford it."

"Wow," Andy said, focusing on a page about the south of France. "That's . . . awesome." Again Andy felt his face get hot. Had he forgotten how to speak like a normal person?

But Travis didn't seem to notice. "I know, I know." He nodded, pushing his longish blond hair off his forehead. "See, I'm gonna start in Paris, then bike around all these incredible châteaus, and then make my way down to the south to beach city. And that's just France."

Andy had never even thought about going to Europe before, but suddenly, hearing Travis talk about it, he realized it sounded amazing. "Need a traveling partner?" he joked.

Travis shrugged, slouching back into the couch.

"Anyone's welcome," he said. Then he sat back up, nodding at something past Andy. "Hey," he called.

Andy slowly turned around. He'd become so interested in Travis's travel plans that he'd almost forgotten he was here to pick up Six. But there she was now, standing in the doorway and looking beautiful in a short black skirt and a body-hugging lilac button-down shirt.

"Hi, Andy," she said, walking toward him.

"Hey." He stood up and gave her a grin.

But then, looking down at her, he noticed that her shirt revealed more than a little bit of cleavage. Six had gone from sporty and unthreatening to sexy and ready in the blink of an eye. Andy swallowed. What did she think was going to happen tonight?

How did I get myself into this? he wondered, shifting his weight from one foot to the other. Andy didn't have an answer for that one. All he knew was that somehow he'd rather sit there and talk to Travis about his trip all night than go out with Six and deal with whatever was to come. That wasn't exactly a promising beginning to a relationship, was it?

"I should be saying something brotherly about now, right?" Travis teased, standing up as well. He patted Andy on the back. "Like, touch my sister and you die."

Six rolled her eyes but smiled. "Very funny, Travis."

Andy forced a laugh, but he couldn't help thinking that at the moment, touching Six was the last thing on his mind. And it was obviously on the fore-front of hers.

He stuck his hands in the front pockets of his khaki pants.

So. What was he supposed to do now?

"This is perfect. Exactly what I felt like doing tonight," Elizabeth Wakefield murmured as she placed the carton of pad Thai down on the glass coffee table in front of her, then nuzzled into Conner McDermott's arms.

"Good," Conner responded, even though *perfect* wasn't exactly the word he would use to describe this night. He and Elizabeth were supposed to go out to dinner together alone, but Elizabeth had nixed that plan. They'd had a late night the night before with all of their friends at the Riot, the club they often frequented, and Elizabeth had had a very long day at Sedona, the cosmetics store where she worked in the Sweet Valley Mall. So when she'd come home a couple of hours earlier, she'd told Conner that she was tired and asked if they could just hang out at her house instead. Conner had said fine, even though it seemed like Elizabeth was always either tired or not around lately. Not to mention that Conner didn't exactly get the most comfortable vibe whenever he was chez Wakefield.

"I mean, what more could I want?" Elizabeth went on, running her fingers over Conner's white-T-shirted chest. "I've got you, some great food, and"—Elizabeth sat up, squinting at the television screen across from them—"and some B-level romantic comedy that never made it to the theaters."

Conner put his own carton of food down on the table and crossed one leg over his knee. His chest still tingled from Elizabeth's touch. "I don't know," he said, "maybe some privacy?"

Elizabeth smiled, setting off a sparkle in her aqua eyes. "I told you—my parents are sleeping. They are *not* going to come downstairs."

Conner dropped his head against the back of the beige couch. He rubbed his eyes with his fists. "Right. And Jessica's—"

"Not coming home for at least an hour," Elizabeth interrupted, pulling Conner's hands away from his face. "She's closing at House of Java tonight." She pinched his side playfully. "Stop being such a downer."

Conner sat up straight, about to snap back at Elizabeth and tell *her* to stop ignoring the fact that he was genuinely annoyed. But as he gazed back at Elizabeth's gorgeous, delicate features, illuminated by the flickering light of the television in the darkened room, he chose to keep that comment to himself.

"Conner?" Elizabeth said, worried creases popping up on her forehead. "I was just kidding. Is something wrong?"

"No." Conner placed a hand on her thigh, touching her soft bare skin where her jean shorts ended. Elizabeth was right. He *was* being a downer, but it had nothing to do with her. He was just worked up because his mom was coming home from rehab in a couple of days, and he knew disaster was sure to ensue. Still, he shouldn't take it out on Elizabeth. He'd done that one too many times already. And she was the one sane thing in his life.

Which was precisely why he wanted to see more of her.

He squeezed her thigh. "But could we do something together tomorrow?" Conner winced, hating the wimpy sound of his voice. What the hell was with him? He sounded like a girl.

"I wish." Elizabeth brought her legs up onto the couch and hugged them, curling her body into a ball as she leaned against the sofa's plump cushions. She put her hand over her mouth, yawning. "But I have to meet with my group for that history project tomorrow, and considering the slackers I'm stuck with, that will probably take hours. And tomorrow night I have a family dinner that I can't get out of."

Conner leaned forward, resting his elbows against his knees. Why was it so extremely difficult to see his girlfriend? And what was the actual point of even bothering to have a girlfriend when she was so busy?

You sound like a needy idiot, Conner thought, running a hand through his scruffy brown hair. Elizabeth's head was resting against the couch's pillow, and her eyes were half closed. She was obviously exhausted from working all day. He was prepared to just drop it, but a voice from somewhere inside him said aloud, "Yeah, well, let me know when you can fit me in."

Elizabeth's eyes popped open wide, and Conner's stomach turned over. He had to get a grip. Pronto.

"I thought we talked about this," she said wearily.

"I know," Conner answered, backing off.

She traced the outline of his ear with her finger. Shivers of pleasure shot through Conner's body. "Why don't we go out on Monday night, after my shift at Sedona?"

Conner looked down at his hands. He felt too stupid to look at her face. How could he have just said that? "Yeah," he responded. "Sure."

He fell back against the couch again, and Elizabeth now settled against his chest. Trying to forget everything that had just happened, Conner closed his eyes, playing with the sleeve of Elizabeth's pink T-shirt.

"Good," Elizabeth whispered. "That'll be nice."

Relaxing, Conner opened his eyes and brought his hand up to her silky blond hair, massaging her head. This was all he needed—some downtime with Elizabeth. Some time to not think about his mom coming home. He stretched out his legs, crossing one over the other. And for a couple of moments, as they were both silently absorbed by the cheesy television movie, he felt calm and tranquil.

"So," Elizabeth said, yawning again. "How's everything going at home?"

Conner sighed. Right back to stressed-out mode. "Well, Megan and I are getting ready for Mom's big arrival," he quipped. "Today we dumped out all of the alcohol in the house."

Silence.

Conner glanced down at Elizabeth's head, which was resting peacefully on his chest. He lifted his eyebrows. She wasn't exactly the silent type.

"Liz?" he said.

Silence again.

He propped himself up a little to look at Elizabeth's face. Sure enough, her eyes were closed, and she looked like she was well on her way to la-la land.

Conner took his hand away from her hair. *Yeah, Liz,* he thought. Perfect *is just the word I'd use to describe tonight.*

Jeremy Aames

Okay, so Jessica has made it perfectly clear that she just wants to be friends with me. And that's fine. I can handle that. Really. After all, having a platonic Jessica in my life is better than no Jessica at all. I'm just going to have to keep to a simple list of rules in order to keep my hormones in check whenever I'm around her.

1. Always maintain a safe distance. If I get close enough to smell her perfume or shampoo, take a step back.

2. Never hang out with Jessica alone in a dark place. Movies are definitely out.

3. Try not to make her laugh. She looks too beautiful when she does.

4. *Don't touch her under any circumstances. No nudging, no tapping, and definitely no hugging.*

Well . . . there might be some exceptions to that last rule. Like, I should be allowed to hug Jessica if she wins the lottery or something.

Or gets an A.

Or successfully makes a tall iced half-caf skim latte.

Wait. A B-plus warrants a hug, doesn't it? What about a B?

Not to mention a bargain purchase at the mall . . .

CHAPTER 2

Not Your Typical High-School Guy

Six was grinning from ear to ear as she and Andy walked to the car after dinner. Andy couldn't help releasing a small smile himself. He'd had a good time, and his doubts from the beginning of the night had vanished. They'd had an incredible dinner at Flamenco, the upscale tapas restaurant that Andy had chosen, and he'd managed to relax with Six, laughing and joking with her all night. Even the weather gods seemed to be on Andy's side. It was a perfect southern California evening—a clear, moon-lit sky with a slight warm breeze.

So what if Six likes me a little more than I like her? Andy reasoned as they approached his car. *I do like her. And that kind of stuff can never be even, can it?*

"I can't believe that place is so close to my house and I'd never been there before," Six said as she waited for Andy to unlock the car. "I mean, the food was awesome."

Andy popped the locks, and they got in. He immediately started the engine. *Yes,* he thought. *Score two points for Marsden.*

"Yeah," he responded nonchalantly, glancing behind him as he backed out of the parking space. "It's one of my favorite restaurants." Andy's voice might sound cool, but on the inside he was totally elated. Sure, he was aware that he had more than his share of flaws, but if there was one thing Andy knew about himself, it was that he had great taste. It was just nice to have that confirmed.

Pulling to a stop at the parking lot's exit, he glanced over at Six. One of her legs was crossed over the other, and he noticed that she had a delicate tattoo of a sun on her tiny left ankle.

Andy mentally patted himself on the back as he made a left out of the parking lot. Apparently he had great taste in women as well.

"There are probably lots of restaurants I don't know about," Six commented. She rolled down her car window, grasping at the air with her hand. "My family never goes out to dinner."

"That's, like, all my family does," Andy said.

"Really?" Six exclaimed. "No one ever cooks?"

Andy laughed. He adjusted his rearview mirror. "Let's just say that mac and cheese is the extent of culinary talents in the Marsden household."

Six giggled. "No way." She shook her head, gathering her strawberry-blond hair into a ponytail. "Well, that settles it, then."

"Settles what?" Andy asked as he turned down the Hansons' street.

"I'm definitely going to come over and give you a

20

cooking lesson. We'll make the Hanson specialty—lasagna."

Andy raised his eyebrows, slowing down as he tried to remember which driveway was Six's. "If you succeed in teaching me how to cook lasagna, I think my mother'll just about insist that we get married."

A heavy silence fell over the car, and Andy felt a blush attack his cheeks instantly. What had he just said? He had to remember that he couldn't just kid around with Six the same way he did with Tia. Because when he was with Six, his lame jokes implied things. Things that he completely didn't mean to say.

Still, Six didn't seem to mind. She lightly touched Andy's knee. "Andy?" she said, her light green eyes suddenly overflowing with mischief. "You wanna park here for a sec?"

Andy's forehead creased in confusion, his palms still sweating from his slip of the tongue. He put the car into park. "But isn't that your driveway up there?"

Six bit her lip. The corners of her mouth curved into a sly smile. "Yeah. That's why I'd like to hang out *here*."

Oh. Right. Andy felt his neck muscles tighten into little balls as Six's face inched closer to his. Obviously she wanted to kiss him. And suddenly Andy wanted to be anywhere but there. *Just kiss her, Marsden,* he told himself. *It's no big deal.*

He closed his eyes and leaned forward, softly

touching his lips to Six's. He kissed her slowly and gently, his body still rooted firmly in his seat. He was just noting the fruity scent of her shampoo when she pulled away.

Andy relaxed, his shoulders slumping. That was sort of . . . nice. And Six looked pleased. Yup. He definitely was the man.

Then Six did something that made Andy's neck go right back to tense position.

After shyly smiling and pushing a lock of hair behind her ear, Six began to unbutton the pearl-colored buttons of her blouse. At first Andy just sat there in shock, not knowing what to do, but when Six unbuttoned her third button, thereby revealing the top of her white cotton bra, Andy panicked.

"Whoa!" he blurted out.

Six jumped, clearly startled, and Andy licked his lips, immediately amending his previous outburst with, "Uh, I don't think we should do this."

Two pink circles popped up on Six's cheeks. Her eyes flashed with hurt. "Why not?"

Yeah, Marsden, why not? Andy placed both hands on the steering wheel and focused on his lap. *Were girls even supposed to do that?* he wondered, his heart hammering. Weren't they supposed to wait for the guy to make the first move or something? *Not that you would,* a tiny voice in the back of his head told him. But still. Why was she so damn forward?

"Because," he told her, his brain searching for an appropriate response. "Because I don't want to get you home too late. I don't want your parents think-ing I'm a jerk."

"Oh," Six mumbled. "Okay."

For a moment Six didn't move, and Andy froze, his hands locked on the steering wheel, not sure of what step to take next. *What would Conner do?* he thought, then shook his head. Conner would have slept with her by now. Man, he definitely needed a manual to tell him how to deal in these situations.

But then Six began to button up her blouse, and Andy felt comfortable enough to put the car back into drive and turn down Six's driveway. Still, he felt like an idiot. How could he turn her down? Why was he so freaked out about all this?

"Hey, Andy?" Six asked as he pulled up to her house.

Andy glanced at her warily. "Yeah?"

She hugged her arms as if she was cold, her eyes focused on her house in front of them. "Are you at-tracted to me?" she asked in a small voice.

Andy's stomach dropped. How could he make this confident, beautiful girl suddenly doubt herself? He looked away, running his fingers up and around the steering wheel.

"Yeah, Six," he told her. "That's not it at all."

Then she asked the inevitable. "So what is it?"

Good question, Andy thought. But he quickly suppressed all of his own doubts, forcing himself to look back at Six and grin.

"It's nothing," he told her in the most reassuring

23

tone he could muster. "Really. It's just that it's only our second real date." He shrugged. "I just think we should take it slow."

The dark cloud that had been hovering over Six's face immediately vanished and was replaced with rays of beaming sunshine.

"Andy!" she said, smiling. "That's so sweet." She grabbed her little black purse up off the floor. "You are such the gentleman." She let out a little sigh, gave Andy a peck on the cheek, then opened the car door. "Talk to you later?"

Andy nodded. "Later."

Six stepped out of the car and then closed the door, jogging up her front path. Andy fell back into his seat, shutting his eyes.

Sure, he was glad that he had successfully convinced Six of his reasons for holding back.

Now if he could just convince himself.

Ken felt an odd sort of déjà vu as he and Maria Slater walked along the beach after dinner at Enzo's on Saturday night. Actually, the déjà vu wasn't exactly that strange, when he considered the fact that he and Maria had walked this very part of the beach at night before, after having dinner at the same exact restaurant that they'd eaten at tonight.

There was only one major difference between that night and tonight. That night Ken had *wanted* to kiss Maria, but he hadn't been ready to. Nor had she given him the go-ahead. And tonight . . . Well, tonight he could just about kiss Maria all he wanted to.

Ken closed his eyes, relishing the feel of the cool ocean breeze blowing through his blond hair and inhaling the salt-infused air. Then he looked over at Maria. Her dark eyes were intensely focused on a space of nothingness before her, her short curls blowing around her face in the wind.

Ken loved how Maria had these two very distinct sides to her personality. At one moment she could be the serious, intense, straight-A Maria that she was now, and the next, the carefree, laughing Maria who wasn't too mature to play hours of miniature golf or get total enjoyment out of eating chili cheese fries from Astro Burger.

Ken clasped her soft hand, squeezing it. Maria turned to look at him, and there she was—the full-of-life Maria, her brown eyes shimmering, her mouth breaking into one of her million-watt smiles.

Man, she was gorgeous.

"I guess I was kind of spacing there, huh?" she said as a particularly large wave crashed behind her.

Ken played with the silver band that she wore on her graceful ring finger, turning it around and around. "Yeah, I was too." In fact, he was still practically in a trance as he gazed back at her, taking in the way the full moon illuminated her smooth, mocha-colored skin and how her loose-fitting cropped sweater and long skirt blew against her slim frame.

He was thinking about how Maria was like medicine for him. Ken had been in a downright crappy mood all day as a result of this morning's frustrating episode, but after just a couple of hours with Maria he felt fine. Happy, even.

As if she could read his mind, Maria tilted her head and said, "Hey. You never finished telling me about what happened with your dad and Asha."

"Oh. Right." Just the mention of it brought Ken's mood right back down. He led Maria over to a spot a couple of feet away and sat, resting his arms on his knees and digging his feet into the cool sand. Maria sat down next to him. "There's not really much more to tell," he said. "Except that Asha was totally pushy and annoying. And oh, man, she's gonna make dinner for us on Monday night. You have to come. There's no way I can be alone with them."

Maria frowned, biting her lip. "I can't. I have to work on Monday."

Ken dropped his head, digging his feet deeper into the sand. "Great," he muttered.

They were both silent for a moment, the only sounds the crashing of the waves and the muted noise of the jazz coming from the restaurant several feet away. Miserable, Ken scooped up some sand and watched it slip through his fingers.

Then Maria sighed. She sat up on both knees. "Okay," she said. "If you really want me to come, I'll find someone to trade shifts with me."

Ken glanced up. "I *really* want you to come."

Maria nodded, brushing a curl away from her eyes. "Then I will. I'll find a way."

"Thank you." Having Maria there was going to make the night so much more bearable. He was just grateful that she'd realized that.

Maria shrugged. "No problem." She nudged his arm playfully. "Besides, now I'll get to judge Asha for myself."

Ken smiled. "Sure," he said. "Whatever."

But that was the last thought concerning Asha that Ken was going to have for the rest of the evening.

Because at present he was moving on to tackle Maria to the ground, kissing her like crazy.

Images from Super Mario land intertwined with visions of Six's hurt expression flashed before Andy's eyes as he lay in his bed, staring up at the paint-chipped ceiling.

Normally, playing a video game was Andy's sure-fire way to extinguish any nagging thoughts or problems from his brain. An hour-long Pokémon session never failed to turn his mind into a useless mound of mush.

Unfortunately, that definitely wasn't the case tonight. Tonight he had played hours of Sega after coming home from his date, hoping to eradicate this evening's strange events from his memory altogether.

But all he could think about was what had happened with Six. Every now and then his thoughts

27

would be interrupted by a flashback of his pathetically played Mario-land game, then he'd go right back to the Six problem. And if he fell asleep, he'd probably have some twisted nightmare in which both he and Six were part of a video game. Like Six would be chasing after Andy with her shirt off as he desperately tried to make his way through the Mario maze.

The thing was, Andy couldn't understand why he *wanted* to run away from Six. Why when she started to take off her shirt, he felt nothing. *Well, not nothing,* he thought, kicking his blue-and-white-striped sheets away from his body. *Try total aversion.*

Andy sat up and leaned against the wall, hugging his pillow to his body. *What the hell's my problem?* he wondered. Wouldn't any warm-blooded American male jump at the chance to make out with a girl, whether they actually liked her or not?

Then Andy tossed the pillow aside. *Wait a minute. . . .* Maybe that was it. Andy wasn't exactly your typical high-school guy. After all, it had taken him until senior year just to get a girlfriend. So it would make sense that he'd want to take the whole sex thing a little slower, right?

Yeah. He was simply on a more leisurely track than most. He probably needed to get to know Six better before he was really attracted to her. That made sense. Andy nodded, grinning to himself. That meant that what he'd said to her tonight wasn't a line of bull. It was the truth.

28

Feeling much better, Andy lay back down and closed his eyes, ready to fall asleep.

He only hoped that visions of Six and Mario would *not* be dancing in his head.

Six Hanson

Six Hanson
Six Marsden
Six Hanson-Marsden
Six Marsden-Hanson
Mrs. Six Marsden
Andy Hanson

"Make me look like Gwyneth Paltrow."

Elizabeth blinked at the short, stocky, brown-haired customer with an unattractive snarl standing on the other side of the glass counter and didn't know what to say. No amount of makeup or magic could transform this woman into the blond actress, but Elizabeth certainly didn't want to be the one to inform her of that. Thankfully, she didn't have to.

"The makeover counter's over there," Elizabeth told the woman, pointing to a petite, red-haired twenty-something woman behind the pink counter in a corner of the store. "Tanya will help you."

The woman grunted and walked away.

Elizabeth forced a smile at the next woman in line, taking black eyeliner and youth-enhancing moisturizer from her to ring them up. Of course, this *would* be the day that Sedona decided to launch a special promotion, causing the line of customers to be literally out the door.

"Fourteen-fifty," Elizabeth told the customer, taking her American Express card.

Elizabeth rubbed her temple as she swiped the credit card. Could this day get any worse?

First she had woken up with a pounding headache, one that was apparently immune to aspirin or Advil. Her head still throbbed now, and the overpowering floral odor of Unique, the perfume that Sedona was currently touting, filled the store, which only made Elizabeth's headache worse. Plus she'd had a more than frustrating day in school. A couple of the members in her history-project group hadn't completed the work they'd promised they would on Sunday, so Elizabeth and Andrea Fertig—the only other responsible member—had to spend their entire lunch period finishing the project for everyone else. Which meant that Elizabeth had gone through the rest of the day starving, having just enough time to grab a veggie burrito in the food court before reporting to work at Sedona. Presently that burrito was having some difficulty settling itself in her stomach, so Elizabeth could now add nausea to the list of her ailments for the day.

Elizabeth gave the woman the receipt for her to sign, took it back from her, and then dropped the complimentary minibottle of Unique into the white plastic bag containing the customer's purchases.

The woman said thank you and walked away. Feeling like she was on autopilot, Elizabeth nodded and smiled at the next customer, taking her items to ring them up.

God, are they really all here just to get their free

sample of Unique? Elizabeth wondered, scanning the never-ending line as the gray-haired woman opened up her lizard purse to pay. *Don't they realize that it smells like a cross between roses and Lysol?*

This day felt as if it were never going to end. And to top it all off, not only had Elizabeth barely seen Conner today, but Carolee, the store's manager, had just asked Elizabeth to work a few extra hours because the store was so packed, which meant that Elizabeth was going to have to cancel her plans with Conner for tonight. She hadn't even had a spare moment to call him and tell him yet. Which seemed ironic, considering that there was a point not long ago when Elizabeth was ditching *everything* for Conner's sake. Part of her wanted to walk out on this job just so that she could spend time with Conner. The only problem was that if she did, her parents would ground her for the rest of her life.

"Here you go," Elizabeth said, handing the woman her cosmetics-stuffed bag. She was just about to grab the next customer's items when she heard a familiar male voice say, "Liz."

Elizabeth glanced to her left, and there Conner was, looking as sexy as ever in his signature white T-shirt and worn-in Levi's. Losing herself in his green eyes for a moment, Elizabeth just smiled and straightened out her calf-length batik-print skirt.

Then she remembered why Conner was here. To pick her up. Elizabeth glanced at her watch. Like, *now.*

"Excuse me?" the fortyish woman at the front of the line suddenly broke in. "I'd like to pay for these?"

"Oh, yes, of course," Elizabeth responded, taking the woman's ridiculous amount of lipstick and nail polish from her.

As Elizabeth quickly rang up all the items, Conner walked closer to the counter. She could feel his eyes on her, waiting. God, she felt so bad that she had to cancel. All she wanted to do was hang out with him anyway.

She ran the woman's credit card through the machine and looked over at him.

"You ready?" he asked, stuffing a hand in his front pocket.

Elizabeth glanced at the still enormous line of customers and bit her lip. "Not exactly." She pushed a strand of her shoulder-length hair behind her ear as she handed the customer her receipt. "It's a zoo here. My boss is making me stay late tonight."

Conner's eyes darkened. "So we can't hang out," he stated, his voice completely flat.

Elizabeth nodded as she handed the woman her bag. "I'm sorry."

"No problem," Conner responded. "I'll just catch you after graduation, then."

Elizabeth's heart twisted as Conner turned, obviously about to leave.

"Wait!" she called after him.

He actually stopped.

"Amber?" Elizabeth said to the tall girl squatted

down on the other side of the circular counter, busily unpacking and restocking shelves in the display cases.

Amber glanced up warily. "Yeah?"

"Could you cover for me for, like, two minutes? I promise I'll be right back."

Amber rolled her big brown eyes, but she stood up, trudging toward Elizabeth.

"Thanks." Elizabeth darted out from behind the counter and over to Conner. "I'm really sorry," she told him again, grabbing both of his wrists.

Conner dropped his head and rubbed his neck. Then, lifting his eyes, he sighed. "It's no big deal, Liz." He stuck his hands in his back pockets. "It's just that my mom's coming home tomorrow and—"

Elizabeth gasped. That's right! She had completely forgotten! Her heart plunged, and she suddenly felt like the worst girlfriend on the planet.

"Conner, I'm so sorry," she said, taking his hand in hers and squeezing it. "I totally forgot."

Conner shrugged. "It's fine."

Elizabeth shook her head, pulling on the hem of his T-shirt. "No, it's not," she told him. "And I'm going to come over as soon as I'm done here."

Conner shrugged again, but this time his eyes brightened a bit. "Okay. Whatever."

"Hey, Liz, we need you over here!" Amber called out in an annoyed tone.

"Looks like you gotta go," Conner said, motioning to Elizabeth's station behind the counter with his head.

35

"Yeah," Elizabeth muttered. "Still have plenty of bad-smelling perfume to give away."

One side of Conner's mouth formed into a smile, and Elizabeth smiled back at him, relieved to see him finally relax. "Well, see you later," she said, standing on her tiptoes to give him a quick kiss.

"Later," Conner said, breaking away.

Amber immediately stepped aside for Elizabeth to take over. "I'll stick to stocking," she whispered before she moved away. "This sucks."

Elizabeth sighed, watching Conner disappear down the mall's elevators.

You can say that again.

Conner sat on the edge of his bed, bouncing his leg and listening to the pouring rain pound against his windows. That, and the occasional explosion of shrill girls' laughter that came from downstairs.

He stood, running a hand through his hair. His narrow bedroom felt tiny and suffocating tonight, but his little sister, Megan, and her two loud best friends, Wendy and Shira, were camped out in the living room downstairs. Conner didn't want to be in the same space as them for a couple of reasons. For one, Wendy and Shira never failed to annoy Conner with the way they stared at and practically drooled after him for hours. Plus tonight they were here helping Megan make dorky signs and chocolate-chip cookies—some sort of a welcome-home surprise for his mom. Conner didn't exactly share his

36

sister's belief that their mother's homecoming was something to celebrate.

After all, their mom had been shipped off by the court because she was a drunk. Okay, sure, she had gone to rehab and everything, but Conner found it hard to believe that his mother—the same woman who couldn't even admit that she *had* a drinking problem—was suddenly going to be cured. *She'll probably walk in here sloshed tomorrow,* Conner thought.

He walked over to the corner of his room and picked up his guitar, then immediately put it back down. He was way too wound up to play. At least Gary, his ex-stepfather, would be out of his face soon. At this very moment Megan's father was packing up his things. *That* was something worth celebrating.

Sighing, Conner walked over to his window and crossed his arms over his chest, watching the thick sheet of rain pound down from the black sky. He knew he had to get out of his house. But it wasn't exactly the kind of night for a walk or a drive. Elizabeth was still at work, and Conner was definitely not in the mood to hang with Andy or Evan.

That left him only one choice. Tia.

No doubt he'd get wet walking over there, but that was better than staying cooped up in his room a second longer. And Tia's house was too close to drive to without looking like an idiot.

Conner pulled his ratty gray fleece jacket out of

his closet and put it on, scribbled a quick note and left it on his bed in case Megan wondered where he was, then slipped out of the house as quietly as possible.

A couple of minutes later, when he was completely soaked and on his way to Tia's, his work boots sinking into the muddy ground and water dripping off his nose, Conner knew he had made the right choice. The rain actually felt good, cooling and kind of liberating, and it was a relief to be out of the confines of his room, where his muddled thoughts crowded his brain.

Conner had been taking the back route to Tia's ever since he was ten, so the fact that it was especially dark on this moonless night didn't matter. He could still find his way perfectly. When Conner reached Tia's window, he barely remembered how he'd gotten there.

Putting his face to the wet glass and peeking in, he saw Tia right away. She was crouched down in front of the VCR with her back to him, sticking a tape in the machine. Conner tapped on the windowpane, and she immediately jumped up. Then slowly she turned around, her hand over her heart. Conner laughed at Tia's bug-eyed brown eyes and the paleness of her normally dark complexion.

She stomped over to the window.

Here it comes, Conner thought. *Tee's tirade.*

Right on cue, Tia opened the window, yelling, "What the hell are you doing? Trying to scare me half to death?"

Conner shrugged, unable to hide his grin. "Wasn't the goal. But it was kind of funny."

Tia shook her head, her long, wavy dark hair falling over her shoulders. "God. I should just leave you out here," she fumed, but then stepped aside so that Conner could crawl through the window. "Have you ever heard of this new piece of technology called the phone?"

"Whatever, Tee. Why were you so scared? I do this all the time." Conner stepped inside her bedroom, dripping water onto her beige carpeting. Her large, pale-colored room felt warm and welcoming after he'd been outside in the downpour. It smelled kind of nice too. Conner couldn't pinpoint the slightly floral scent exactly—he just knew it was a smell he associated with Tia.

"Yeah," Tia responded. "But never in a torrential downpour."

Conner shrugged. "It was easier to just walk over."

"Really?" Tia looked him up and down, taking in his drenched attire. "Yeah. I can see that."

Conner rolled his eyes. "Could you just get me a towel, Tee?"

Tia threw her hands up in the air. "Oh, sure. First you scare me, then you order me around." But she walked into her bathroom just the same.

As Conner dropped down onto the plush carpet, taking off his shoes, he thought about how this was textbook Tia. She needed to be all dramatic about everything, but in the end, he knew she was psyched that he had come over. She simply found it more fun to act all annoyed. Which was fine with him. Tia's dramatics were just the kind of distraction he needed tonight.

Tia reemerged from the bathroom, holding a fluffy white towel. "Here you are, master," she quipped, handing it to him.

Conner took the towel and scrubbed his short brown hair dry. As he did so, he looked at Tia and noticed what she was wearing: a worn-in gray El Carro football sweatshirt that was so big on her, it fit her like a dress, coming down to her knees. Conner smiled. The way her tiny little body swam in that sweatshirt, she looked like she was twelve.

"What?" Tia asked, meeting Conner's eyes. Then she glanced down at herself and sighed. "I know, I know, I shouldn't still be wearing Angel's stuff," she said, referring to her ex-boyfriend. "But this is too cozy. I can't help it."

Conner shrugged. "I don't think it's a big deal."

Tia's dark eyebrows scrunched together. "You don't?" Conner shook his head. Tia bit her lip, her hands disappearing inside her ridiculously long sleeves. "Yeah. You're right. Who cares?" Then she plopped down across from Conner Indian style, her sweatshirt covering her legs. "So, what's the occasion for this visit?" she asked. "Did you just *have* to see me?"

"Yeah. That, and my mom's coming home to-morrow." Conner glanced down. He fiddled with his work boot's soaked shoelace. "I couldn't deal with my house tonight. I had to get out."

"Oh." Tia's large, dark eyes searched his face for a moment. Then she stood up and broke into a smile, her trademark dimples popping up on both sides. "In that case, this is perfect. I was just about to watch *Ferris Bueller's Day Off*. You ready to have your butt kicked?"

Conner's mouth curved into a grin. He and Tia always had competitions over who knew more lines in the movie. This was just the type of mindless activity he needed. He tossed the towel at Tia's head. "You are going down tonight."

"In your dreams." Tia laughed, standing up and throwing the towel back at him. She walked over to her cherry-stained bureau on the other side of the room and opened up the middle drawer, pulling out a pair of blue sweatpants. She tossed them over to Conner. "Put these on. They'll fit—they're Angel's too," she told him. "I'll go get the necessary supplies." Then she jogged out of the room.

Conner took off his wet jeans and pulled on Angel's sweatpants. He knew that the "supplies" Tia was referring to were a Mallomar apiece and popcorn—their standard movie-viewing snacks.

Yeah, Conner thought, making himself comfortable on Tia's four-poster bed. *This was definitely the right move.*

Ken glanced around his wood-paneled dining room in amazement. To begin with, he was shocked that they were actually going to *eat* in this room. He and his father hadn't eaten a meal here since his parents' divorce a couple of years ago. On the nights that he and his father did eat dinner together, they ate in the kitchen, and more often than not with the tiny kitchen television set turned to ESPN.

The second reason for Ken's shock was the way the maple dining-room table looked. Asha had set the table with silver-trimmed plates and gleaming silverware that Ken didn't even know they had. Not to mention the pale blue cloth napkins and carved wooden napkin rings. Where had *those* come from? Plus Asha had brought over some sunflowers, which she had arranged in a tall, painted ceramic vase that Ken could swear he'd never seen before.

Huh, Ken thought. *Maybe having Asha around won't be* so *bad.* After all, Ken could deal with living in a clean house.

And he could also deal with home-cooked food. Ken walked into the kitchen and was welcomed by the stomach-growling scent of sautéing garlic and onions. Maria and Asha were standing side by side with their backs to him, cutting vegetables on the countertop. They were almost the same exact height—Maria in her Skechers and Asha in her strappy brown sandals—and with their similar slender builds, they looked like they could be sisters.

"I started out as an editorial assistant for the *Valley Observer,*" Asha was saying as she effortlessly chopped a yellow pepper into tiny pieces, "and I kept getting promoted there until I became a news reporter. Then I switched over to the *Tribune*."

"So you just worked your way up?" Maria asked as she rinsed off a tomato in the sink. "That's so cool."

Asha laughed. "Trust me. It's not nearly as exciting as it sounds."

Ken stood in the doorway and watched them, suddenly feeling uncomfortable. Sure, Maria was always good with people and everything, but it seemed like the two of them were already totally buddy-buddy. Ken knew that he should be glad that Maria and Asha were getting along, but for some reason, it bothered him. Especially when he thought about the fact that his own mother hadn't even met Maria yet.

Maria glanced over her shoulder and noticed Ken. "Hey, there." She tossed some diced tomatoes into the wooden salad bowl in between her and Asha, then wiped her hands on a dishrag. "I was just telling Asha about how I might want to go into journalism one day."

"Oh," Ken said, taking another step into the kitchen. He didn't really feel like getting involved in their getting-to-know-you conversation. "Right."

"What about you, Ken?" Asha asked as she walked over to the stove. Grabbing the yellow pot holder, she lifted the lid of the cast-iron pot that the tomato sauce was cooking in and peered inside. "Do you know what you want to do?"

It took all of Ken's strength not to roll his eyes. He was seventeen, and he was supposed to have his life figured out? Even worse, he was supposed to share that information with Asha? "No," he grunted. Out of the corner of his eye he saw Maria shoot him a look as she peeled a cucumber, but he ignored it. Maria could divulge her life story to Asha if she wanted, but that didn't mean Ken had to.

"Well, you still have plenty of time," Asha offered, wiping her hands on the red apron that was tied around her waist.

Ken didn't respond. He didn't need any of Asha's advice or words of wisdom.

"So," Maria said quickly. "What's left to do?" She tossed the cucumber slices into the salad bowl.

Asha surveyed the kitchen. "Not much, really," she said, pushing a strand of wavy dark hair away from her eye. "We shouldn't start the pasta until Ed gets home." She glanced at her silver-link watch, which hung loosely on her narrow wrist, and frowned. "Actually, I thought he'd be here by now."

And I *thought he was going to come to my awards dinner. How funny.* Ken walked over to the counter and grabbed a piece of red pepper from the salad bowl, popping it into his mouth. "Yeah, well, Dad's not exactly known for his punctuality."

Another look from Maria. Ken shrugged at her. What was the crime? He was just telling the truth. Asha should know what she was getting herself into.

The phone rang, and Ken walked over to pick up

44

the receiver, eager to put some space between him and Maria's annoyed glare. "Hello?"

"Ken," his father said. "It's Dad."

"Oh. Hey," Ken responded. "Are you coming home soon?"

Mr. Matthews let out a sigh on the other side of the line. "Unfortunately, no. I'm not going to make dinner."

"What? Why not?" Ken asked. Out of the corner of his eye he saw Asha's eyebrows shoot up in surprise.

"I'm in LA, covering the Lakers game. It doesn't look like I'm gonna be leaving anytime soon," he explained.

"Oh." Ken wrapped the phone cord tightly around his finger. He'd heard this before. His father often bailed on plans because of work.

"You guys have fun without me, all right?"

With *his* girlfriend? "Yeah." Ken kicked at the molding on the edge of the wall. "Sure."

"Good," Mr. Matthews replied. "Well, gotta run. Tell Asha I'll call her later."

"Okay." Ken paused for a moment before hanging up the phone. As he listened to the dial tone on the other end, he silently wished he'd told his father that he should be the one to explain to Asha why he was blowing her off, not Ken.

But you didn't, Ken thought, *so you better get this over with.* Maybe she'd decide to leave. Then Ken wouldn't have to deal with her anymore.

But when he finally turned around and looked at Asha, he was hit by a sudden wave of guilt. Asha was staring at the floor, picking at her nails, her mouth a

45

straight line. A portrait of disappointment.

Ken tugged at his collar. "Uh, Dad can't get away from work," he said. "But he said he'd call you later."

Asha looked up and nodded slightly. Her brown eyes, which had seemed so lively moments before, now looked flat.

"Okay," she said, managing an obviously forced smile. She let out a heavy breath and picked up the box of spinach linguine. "Well," she went on in a false cheery voice, "guess we should put the pasta on, then."

Ken and Maria shared a look as Asha walked over to the stove. Thankfully, Maria's glare of annoyance had softened into one of sympathy, but Ken still felt like the most immature guy on the planet.

I shouldn't have been so rude to Asha, Ken realized, his cheeks flaming up. After all, she was just a woman who happened to be dating his father.

It wasn't *her* fault that his father was a jerk.

"What time is your mom coming home?" Tia asked, sitting up and scooping out the marshmallow part of a Mallomar with her tongue as she looked down at Conner.

Conner rubbed his eyes with his hands, feeling like his head was sinking deeper into Tia's mass of enormous, lacy down pillows. The muted sounds of *Ferris Bueller* could be heard from the TV in front of the bed, but they'd stopped watching it a while ago. And he wasn't exactly sure how they had gotten on the subject of his mom, but for once, he didn't mind talking about her.

"I don't know," he muttered, dropping his hands down on either side of him. "I guess sometime in the afternoon."

Tia finished up her cookie, then quickly closed the Mallomar box and reached over Conner's legs to put it down on the floor. "You know, rehab can work," she said. "Your mom really might be better."

Conner sat up a little, propping himself up on the pillows. "That's doubtful." He focused on the flashing images of the TV with clouded eyes, not really absorbing anything he was seeing. "My mom manages to screw most things up."

They were both silent for a moment, fake watching the movie, until Tia lightly touched Conner's leg. "It's hard to know what'll happen, Conner," she said, staring into his eyes. "But I'm sure you'll be able to handle this. No matter what."

Conner glanced down and let out a heavy breath. How could she be so sure? *Because I always* do *handle this crap*, he thought. He picked up a pillow, fidgeting with its lace trimming. "That's the thing," he said, turning the pillow over and over again in his hands. "I mean, yeah, I always keep it together. But it's getting old, Tee." He looked up at her, meeting her wide-eyed gaze. "I don't how much longer I can do it."

"I'm sure you've felt that way before," she responded, hugging her knees to her chest. "And you've always pulled through." She rested her chin on her knees, so that all Conner could see of her face were her brown eyes and wide forehead. "You will this time too."

"Yeah, but this time—," Conner began, then abruptly broke off, gripping the pillow tightly. "Whatever."

"No," Tia said, lifting her head. "What were you going to say?"

Conner stared down at the square white pillow. The air in the room suddenly felt thick. He couldn't hear the TV at all anymore—all he could hear was his heart pounding in his ears.

"I'd never tell this to anyone but you," he mumbled, "but . . . I'm actually kind of . . ." He looked back up at Tia. "Freaked out."

Tia leaned in closer to Conner, holding on to his arm. "You mean scared?"

Oh, man, what had he just said? Conner swore silently at himself, his eyes darting back down to the pillow. He felt a blush slowly crawl up from his neck. Still, he managed a quiet "Maybe."

And then the densest, heaviest silence that Conner had ever experienced filled the room. He couldn't get himself to lift his eyes to look Tia in the face.

Until he heard, "Hey, guys!"

Elizabeth's "Hey, guys!"

She was standing in Tia's doorway, looking from Conner to Tia with obvious surprise in her sea green eyes.

Conner threw down the pillow and jumped up off the bed at the sight of her, his mind reeling over what he had just told Tia.

Man, if Elizabeth heard . . . , he thought, feeling his face get even hotter.

"Liz, hi," Tia said, looking as startled as Conner felt.

Get it together, he ordered himself. "Uh, hey," he managed, going to stick his hands in his front jeans pockets, then realizing that he was still wearing Angel's sweatpants. "What're you doing here?"

Elizabeth stepped into the room, glancing in confusion from Tia to Conner. "Looking for you," she explained, twisting her silver necklace around her finger. "Megan told me you were here." She focused on Conner's sweatpants, then glanced back up at his face. "Conner? What's going on?"

"What do you mean?" he asked, running a hand through his hair. "Tee and I were just hanging out."

"Talking," Tia added.

Elizabeth glanced down at her black leather sandals and nodded. "Then why are you acting so weird?" she asked in a quiet voice.

Maybe because you couldn't have picked a worse moment to barge in here, Conner thought. But he just shrugged. "We weren't expecting you."

Elizabeth again focused on the sweatpants. "Whose are those?"

Conner rolled his eyes, his hands balling into fists. He was uncomfortable with this scene. Too uncomfortable. He wished he'd never come over here. "God, Liz, what's with all the questions?" he asked. "They're Angel's."

"Conner borrowed them from me," Tia supplied quickly. "Because his were wet." She tugged on the bottom of her sweatshirt, pulling it down. "I mean, from the rain."

"Oh," Elizabeth said, still not sounding completely convinced. She stared at Conner. "I guess I just thought that *we* were going to hang out tonight."

Conner sighed. What was her deal? "We were. And then you had to work late. Remember?"

Elizabeth's cheeks flushed pink, and she shook her head. Finally her face relaxed. "God, I'm sorry," she told them. "I don't know what's wrong with me. Of course you guys were just hanging out."

"Right," Conner said. He could feel Tia's gaze on him, but he shook it off. He figured that she thought he should tell Elizabeth what they'd been talking about, but that was *not* going to happen. He had to get out of the intensity of this room. Now.

"I'm gonna put these back on," he said, walking over and picking up his jeans. "Then you wanna drive me home?"

Elizabeth nodded. "Sure."

"Cool." Jeans in hand, Conner walked into Tia's bathroom and shut the door. He sat down on the closed toilet and scrunched his eyes closed.

That was not a fun moment. He was just glad that he'd been able to cut Elizabeth's little game of twenty questions short. And that Elizabeth hadn't tried to make him tell her what he and Tia had been talking about.

Because *that* he couldn't handle.

Cherie Reese

To: foxy@swiftnet.com
From: cherier@swiftnet.com
Subject: Help!

Liss:

Did you finish the calc homework? Can I copy it? I totally don't get it and can't deal with trying to anymore.

How was the movie? Should I see it?

Oh God, did you hear about Scott Brennan and Bria Mandel? How could he go out with her? Ick.

btw, speaking of undesirable females, the word is that Jessica Wakefield is officially single. Watch out. It's only a matter of time before she goes after Will—again!

Later—

xo Cherie

melissa Fox

To: cherier@swiftnet.com
From: foxy@swiftnet.com
Subject: Whatever

Cherie:
   Okay. I'll answer your questions in order.
   1. Yes. You can copy it tomorrow before homeroom.
   2. Will loved the movie, I didn't. I wouldn't see it unless you're interested in simply watching Cameron Diaz look gorgeous for two straight hours.
   3. Are you sure you're not jealous? If I remember correctly, you and Scott shared a smooch freshman year. . . .
   4. Don't worry about me. I'm sure Will will never stray again.
   Good night.
                    Melissa

CHAPTER
Kind of a Conflict

4

Ken glanced up from his overflowing bowl of corn-flakes at the sound of his father's footsteps coming down the stairs on Tuesday morning. Slowly sipping his orange juice, he tried to think of what he should say to his dad. All he knew was that he had to say *something*.

The thing was, the more he thought about what had happened last night, the less sense it made. When Asha had brought up the dinner suggestion on Saturday morning, why hadn't his father mentioned that he had to cover a game in LA that night? Didn't he realize that that was kind of a conflict? And besides, his father was a senior sports editor. There were plenty of other reporters who would have done the coverage for him if he'd asked. So why *didn't* he ask?

Ken still didn't know how he felt about his father and Asha dating, but he had learned a couple of things last night. For one, Asha wasn't a bad person, and for another, she didn't deserve to be treated badly—by Ken *or* his father.

"Morning," Mr. Matthews said, walking into the kitchen.

"Morning, Dad," Ken responded, watching his father as he took the grapefruit juice out of the refrigerator and poured himself a glass. Ken pushed around his cereal with his spoon for a moment. "So, you got in late last night, huh?"

His father nodded as he drank. "Helluva game. Went into overtime." He opened up the fridge again, this time pulling out the package of English muffins.

"Did you talk to Asha?" Ken ventured, helping himself to a spoonful of now very soggy flakes.

Mr. Matthews gave Ken a questioning look for a second, his blue eyes narrowing. "Yeah," he said, crossing his arms over his chest. "Called her when I got home. She said you guys had a nice dinner."

No thanks to you, Ken thought. "We did. She seems cool, Dad."

Ken's father nodded almost imperceptibly at the compliment. He took another gulp of his grapefruit juice.

Ookay, Ken thought. "But we were bummed that you couldn't make it," he went on, watching his father carefully.

Mr. Matthews's blond eyebrows lifted in surprise. He placed his glass down on the counter. "Well, so was I. That's why it's called work."

Ken looked down at his bowl. Somehow that wasn't exactly the response he was looking for. He glanced back up at his father. "But couldn't you have asked a reporter to take your place at the game? I mean, there are so many—"

"If I could, don't you think I would've?" Mr. Matthews interrupted. His muffin slices popped up in the toaster, and he angrily pulled them out. "It's my job, Ken. I can't just leave whenever I want, as convenient as that would be."

Ken blinked, watching his dad grab the cream cheese out of the fridge. "Yeah, but I mean, didn't you know about the game for a while?" he asked finally, standing up and walking closer to his father. "'Cause on Saturday—"

"Enough!" Ken's father cut in, his entire face, including his earlobes, turning pink. "What's with all the questions?"

Ken swallowed, taking a step back. His dad had never lost it like that on him. But then again, they hardly ever spoke about anything anyway. Maybe there was another way to talk about this. "It's just that Asha seemed kind of disappointed last night and—"

"Really?" Mr. Matthews interrupted again, nodding with a vengeance. "Well, I see." Turning his back on Ken, he tore a paper towel off the roll on the counter and stuck his muffin on it.

Ken winced. It seemed like there was no way his father would calm down now that he was all worked up.

"But if it's all right with you," Mr. Matthews went on, "I'll deal with my personal business myself. You can just stay out of it." And then, without giving Ken so much as a second glance, he stormed out of the kitchen and out of the house, slamming the front door behind him.

Letting out a shaky breath, Ken listlessly picked up the tub of cream cheese and put it back in the refrigerator. His eyes fell on the pots that sat in the drying rack next to the sink, and he thought back to last night and how Asha had managed to make this place feel like a home for the first time in years.

Ken sank back down into his chair, contemplating his bowl of cereal.

Maybe having Asha around was exactly what they needed.

"Give your mom my best wishes."

Yeah, right. Just go home to Seattle and your teenage fiancée, Conner thought as he watched Gary hug Megan good-bye.

Megan nodded, her green eyes cast downward. "I will," she said, pulling away from her father.

Conner's heart tightened as he saw Megan bite her lip and twist a strand of her wavy red hair around her finger, clearly trying to fight back the tears. As glad as Conner was to see Gary go, he knew how tough it was for his sister to say good-bye.

"I'll call you in a couple of days," Gary said. Then he glanced at Conner. Nodding, Gary ran a hand over his bald head, not bothering to come any closer to him, for which Conner was grateful. "You take care," he said.

Conner folded his arms over his chest, lifting his

chin. "Yeah, Gary. You too." *Now just go,* he added silently.

Gary looked back at Megan. "Okay, then." He lifted his battered brown-and-beige suitcase off the floor. "I'd wait around for your mom, but I've got a plane to catch."

Megan nodded solemnly. "I know." She reached up and gave him one last kiss on the cheek.

And that was it. Megan opened the front door, and Gary walked out, suitcase in hand—Conner sure as hell wasn't going to offer to carry it for him—and got into his Lexus, which was parked at the curb.

Megan watched Gary disappear into the car, then closed the front door.

"You okay, Sandy?" Conner asked.

"Yeah," she answered, without looking at him. "I'm fine." Sighing, she dropped her hands at her sides and wandered over to the staircase, sinking down on the first step. "Thank God Mom's coming home today," she said quietly, picking at a loose thread in her wide-legged white cotton pants.

Conner walked over and sat down next to her. He didn't want to bum Megan out any more than she already was, but he also couldn't fake enthusiasm about his mom's return. Not when he was filled with a nauseating sense of uneasy dread whenever he thought about what her homecoming might bring.

He put his hand on Megan's head, messing up her long hair. "Everything's going to be fine," he told her, even though he didn't quite believe it himself.

Megan glanced at him with painfully young-looking eyes. "I know," she began. "I just—" She broke off as they heard the sound of a car pulling into their driveway. Her eyes immediately transformed, sparkling with excitement. "That's probably her!" she exclaimed, jumping up and running over to the window by the front door. She pushed aside the white curtain and peeked outside. "It is! It's Mom!"

Conner slowly stood and walked over to the front door as Megan ran outside.

"Mom! You're early!" he heard her yell cheerfully. He watched her jog over and greet their mother, hugging her and then helping her to get her monogrammed suitcase out of the taxi's trunk.

Conner squinted at them, hanging back, trying to take this all in. He just couldn't run up to his mother the way Megan had and pretend to be the loving son after everything that had happened.

His mom looked the same, basically. Still tall and a tad overweight. She wore a familiar pair of black pants with a crisp blue button-down shirt, and her blond hair was pulled back into a bun the way it usually was. Actually, she looked tanned (well, as tanned as someone as pale as her was capable of getting) and healthy. More like she'd been at a spa than at a rehab center.

Conner shook his head. There's no way his mom would look that relaxed if she wasn't still downing the vodka.

But as she came closer, Conner did note a change in her facial expression. He couldn't exactly put his finger on it, but it just seemed that she appeared less perfectly composed, less . . . certain.

"Conner," she said softly as she approached.

"I'll bring this to your room." Megan beamed, walking past them.

"Hi, Mom," Conner said flatly. He didn't mean to sound as harshly cold as he knew he had. He just couldn't help it.

"Hi," she said, leaning in to give him a quick, almost fearful hug.

Conner simply stared back at her. He didn't know what to say.

"Conner, I'm sorry for what's happened," she told him quietly, searching his face with watery blue eyes. "But I promise, things are going to get better around here."

Conner felt his stomach twist and turn. His mom had made plenty of promises in the past, and she had broken all of them. Why would things be any different now? "Yeah," he said. "Okay."

Mrs. Sandborn opened her mouth as if she was going to say something more but then closed it. "We'll catch up later," she said finally, giving him a weak smile. Then she walked off toward her room.

Conner sighed and closed the front door.

She can say whatever she wants, he thought. *I'll believe it when I see it.*

*   *   *

"Want one?" Tia asked Elizabeth as she dipped a nacho chip into the little container of very Velveeta-like orange cheese.

"No, thanks," Elizabeth said, cringing inwardly at Tia's pseudo-Mexican food. It reminded her of that veggie burrito she'd eaten yesterday afternoon. The veggie burrito that she was practically still tasting today.

The resemblance shouldn't have surprised her since both food items came from the same source: Burrito Palace in the Sweet Valley Mall's food court. A few minutes earlier Tia had surprised Elizabeth by showing up at Sedona, so Elizabeth had taken a break to hang out with her for a little while. Now the two of them were sitting at one of the red square plastic tables next to the Palace's counter, Tia munching away on her nachos and Elizabeth sipping a megasized root beer.

Elizabeth sat back in her chair and fidgeted with her straw, feeling preoccupied. As much as she knew it was silly, she still couldn't get over the nagging feeling that she had interrupted something when she'd gone over to Tia's. The fact that Conner had been silent and withdrawn when she'd driven him home last night, and again today at school, didn't ease her worries.

He's just anxious about his mom coming home, she argued with herself. *Stop being so paranoid.*

"I wonder how everything's going with Conner's mom," she said to Tia, sighing. "I feel so bad for not being there for him last night."

"Nah. Don't worry about it," Tia said casually, popping another chip into her mouth. "He's okay."

"Oh." Elizabeth leaned forward and took a giant gulp of her root beer. Something really bothered her about the way Tia had said "he's okay." She sounded so authoritative—like she really knew. *Like she knows better than me,* Elizabeth thought, staring at her friend as she dipped another nacho in cheese.

But then she immediately felt stupid again. After all, Tia was the one who'd hung out with Conner last night. And as much as that inexplicably got to her, it was Elizabeth's fault. *She* was the one who couldn't make time for Conner, not the other way around, even though for some reason it felt that way to her now.

Feeling a sudden chill from the mall's frigid air-conditioning, Elizabeth took her black cardigan off the back of her chair and pulled it on over her floral-print sundress.

"So," she began, pausing to take another quick sip of soda, "what did you guys talk about last night anyway?"

Tia glanced up from her chips, her dark eyebrows lifting. "Who? Conner and I?"

Elizabeth laughed. A laugh that clearly sounded more nervous than genuine. Her cheeks flushed. "No. You and your little brother. Of course you and Conner."

Tia's brown eyes darted back down to the table. "I don't know. Not much." She shrugged, then pulled

61

a green scrunchie off her wrist. "Music. His mom."

"His mom?" Elizabeth moved to the edge of her little plastic seat. "What did he say?" she pressed, unable to disguise her desperate curiosity.

Tia appeared to be thinking something over as she wrapped the scrunchie around her long dark hair, pulling it into a ponytail. "Oh, nothing major," she said finally. "Don't worry about it."

Don't worry about it? What was that supposed to mean? And why was Tia acting all secretive about this? They were talking about Conner—*her* boyfriend. Why would he confide in Tia instead of Elizabeth?

She shifted in her seat. Okay, sure, she knew Tia and Conner had been friends, like, forever. But still. Conner should come to Elizabeth first. And neither he nor Tia should put Elizabeth in the position of begging Tia for information. Right?

Elizabeth watched as Tia nonchalantly finished up her chips. *And why,* Elizabeth wondered, *does she look kind of* happy *about all of this?*

"But you guys seemed so serious when I walked in last night," Elizabeth tried, wrapping her hands around her paper cup. "Were you talking about his mom then?"

Again Tia shrugged. She pushed her carton of nachos away from her, then grabbed a little napkin out of the metal dispenser in the middle of the table and wiped the corners of her mouth. "I can't remember," she said. "Maybe."

"Oh," Elizabeth mumbled. She could just tell Tia was lying. For one, the girl was completely avoiding eye contact, looking everywhere *around* Elizabeth but not *at* her. Plus she was now fidgeting like crazy, pulling the scrunchie out of her hair and rearranging it three different times.

I can't stand this, she thought. In a sudden movement Elizabeth stood up, glancing at her watch. "I better get back."

"Okay," Tia responded. "Hey, watch out for that Unique stuff. My mom came home with it last night, and it is nasty."

Elizabeth forced a smile. "Yeah. I know." She picked up her black purse from the table. "See you tomorrow."

Tia smiled. "Tomorrow, *chica.*"

Elizabeth quickly turned around, rushing to head back to Sedona. The truth was, she still had time left on her break. But sitting there with Tia, she was feeling increasingly nauseous.

And something told her it had nothing to do with the veggie burrito.

Megan Sandborn

Dad's gone for good.

Am I sad? Kind of. But more at the way things turned out than at the fact that he actually left. Sure, he promised to come out and visit a lot and to call me every week, but I'm not going to hold my breath. I'm not <u>that</u> naive.

I've learned my lesson. I'm not going to be suckered again. I'm not going to expect anything from him. And if he does visit, if he does call me all the time, well, fab. But if not, it won't be like I was actually expecting him to or anything.

Still, I refuse to be like Conner and see the negative in every aspect of life. Dad might be gone, but Mom's home. For good. And I know things are going to be so much better now that she went to rehab.

So Conner can mope around all he wants. I'll be hanging out with Mom.

AN ITTY-BITTY SOMETHING

Conner slowly wandered down the stairs, cursing himself for agreeing to stay home for dinner. That afternoon he'd managed to avoid the whole homecoming scene that Megan had created for their mother, holing himself up in his room while his mother admired the posters and chocolate-chip cookies and whatever other crap that his sister had made. He had nothing to do with it, and he wanted there to be no mistake about it.

But when Megan had knocked on his door a couple of hours earlier, meekly asking Conner to *please* have dinner at home because it would just mean *so* much to their mother . . . Well, Conner couldn't say no.

He really didn't feel like pretending everything was hunky-dory now that his mom was back. Didn't feel like pretending that the past never happened.

Maybe I'll still bail anyway, he thought, taking a heavy step toward the kitchen. Then suddenly his nostrils were filled with a scent that made him stop in place, right in the middle of the hallway. It was the smell of fried chicken. Of his mom *cooking* fried chicken. Conner stood there frozen for a moment, inhaling the greasy but completely mouthwatering scent, closing his eyes and trying to determine if he was right.

Yup. There was no doubt about it. Conner knew the smell all too well. His mother used to make fried chicken all the time when he was little. *Like every week,* Conner thought, *she'd make chicken and mashed potatoes. . . .*

Conner's eyes flew open. He was not going to let himself take that little trip down memory lane, back to the days when his mother wasn't an alcoholic. *That's probably why she's bothering to cook for the first time in years anyway,* he thought, wandering over to the kitchen. *So that I'll remember what she used to be like and forget about everything else.*

Still, he couldn't stop himself from standing in the doorway and silently watching in shock as his mother transferred the pieces of fried chicken onto a porcelain serving platter. The thing was, she didn't look all that different than she had about ten years ago, when Conner was little and this meal was a staple in his life. She was a few pounds heavier and had developed some wrinkles at the corners of her blue eyes, and she now curled her naturally straight blond hair. But that was it. Looking at her, he had trouble believing she really *was* that different.

She is, though, Conner reminded himself, his focus clouding as he was lost in miserable thoughts. *She's totally different.*

Mrs. Sandborn had turned from the stove to place the steaming platter on the table when she noticed Conner.

"Hi," she said, obviously startled. The platter began to slip from her fingers a bit, but she got a hold on it before it fell. She grasped onto it with a supertight grip, her knuckles turning white.

Conner stuck his hands in his front pockets. He didn't really know what to say with his mom acting so nervous around him. It was completely unlike her. "Hey," he mumbled.

She looked at him for a moment without saying a word. Then, as if she suddenly remembered that she had the platter in her hands, she glanced down and said, "Oh!"

She hurried over to the table and placed the chicken on a bamboo place mat in the center. Then she wiped her hands on her off-white apron that said Kiss the Cook! in red letters.

She motioned over to the table with her eyes and gave Conner a tentative smile. "You used to love fried chicken," she said, watching him carefully.

Conner's eyes fell to the linoleum floor.

"Conner," she began, this time in a more serious-sounding voice. A voice that sounded more like her. He glanced up. "I know that one dinner can't make up for the last few years."

Got that right, he thought, glaring at her.

"But I wanted to do something special," she went on, fidgeting with the edge of her apron. "Something to show that we're off to a new start."

She might have sounded convincing to an amateur, but Conner knew better. "Okay, Mom." He shrugged. "Whatever."

He thought he saw a flash of disappointment register in her light blue eyes, and part of him was glad. She'd disappointed him plenty over the years. But then another part of him didn't feel so glad. That half of him felt kind of . . . empty.

"Dinner smells awesome!" Megan exclaimed, appearing seemingly out of nowhere and bursting inside past Conner.

Mrs. Sandborn's face lit up in an instant. "Well, good," she said, grinning at Megan. "That's the point. And it's ready, so why don't we sit down?" She shot Conner a glance, as if she was making sure he'd join them.

Conner sighed as he followed his mother and sister and sat down across from Megan, who was already eagerly helping herself to a large mound of garlic mashed potatoes. Conner's mom poured ice water from a ceramic pitcher into all of their glasses, then took the seat in between Conner and Megan, at the head of the table.

"I can't tell you how badly I was craving this," she said, taking a wing and putting it on her flower-rimmed plate. "The food at the Parker Center was so horrible."

Megan's nose crinkled. "Really?" she asked, carefully selecting a piece of chicken for herself.

Of course. Now we get to hear about the horrors of

70

rehab—bad food and all. Conner reached over to the platter and grabbed a drumstick, and his mom smiled.

"I knew that's what you'd take."

Conner didn't respond. Was it really so shocking that his mother knew what kind of chicken he liked?

"Anyway, yes," his mom went on, looking at Megan. "I lived on peanut butter and jelly. But let's not talk about that. Tell me about soccer. How's your team doing?"

"Killer," Megan said, swallowing a bite of mashed potatoes. "We've won almost every game."

Conner bit into his chicken and was amazed for more than one reason. To begin with, he was surprised that his mother had so quickly moved the topic of conversation away from herself. Normally she could talk about herself for hours, especially if she'd been away. Not to mention the fact that most of the time she'd be too out of it to remember any important aspects of her kids' lives. And on top of it, the chicken tasted even better than he'd remembered. He glanced at his mother as she lifted her glass. It was hard to believe that she hadn't cooked in years. But then again, maybe it was the kind of thing you couldn't forget how to do.

Mrs. Sandborn lifted one sculpted eyebrow as she sipped her water. "Well, just try to keep your injured list down, all right?" she said to Megan in a teasing voice. "I don't need all these mothers calling me and telling me that their daughters have been bruised by you again."

Conner couldn't help cracking a smile at that.

71

His sister was a force to be reckoned with on the field. So much so that a lot of the girls on the opposing teams were afraid of her.

Megan grinned. "Hey," she said, picking at an extra-crispy piece of chicken. "If they can't take the heat—"

"Get out of the game," Conner and his mom both finished for her at the same time.

Megan and Mrs. Sandborn laughed—but Conner didn't. Catching his mom's amused eye, Conner glanced down at his plate, feeling uncomfortable.

What's going on here? he thought, pushing his mashed potatoes around with his fork. He had to keep his distance. Keep his cool.

"Guess I've said that before," Megan joked.

"Just a couple of times," Conner's mom responded. "So. What else is going on around here? How are the lovely Rothchilds?" she asked, referring to their evil elderly neighbors. "Have they killed the Wongs' poodle yet?"

Again Conner couldn't help allowing a small smile. He hadn't seen his mother this with it in years.

"I think they realize there'd be too many witnesses to the crime," he responded. "Everyone's watching them and waiting." His mother and sister laughed again, and he sat back in his seat, stretching out his legs and relaxing a little.

And for just one moment he allowed himself to forget how important it was to keep his distance.

*   *   *

"Uh, Liz? You're not going to put that color on *me,* are you?"

Elizabeth glanced down at the blush Maria was referring to and blinked. It was a light rosy color and totally unsuitable for Maria's dark brown skin.

"Oh, no," she said, hurriedly switching it with the blush she'd meant to pick up. She dipped a yellow makeup sponge into the powder and reached out to apply it to the upper parts of Maria's cheeks.

Maria retracted in her tall wooden stool. "Maybe I should get someone else to do this," she suggested.

"Maria, I'm never going to get better if I don't practice," Elizabeth protested in a whisper so that none of the other Sedona employees or customers would hear.

It was Elizabeth's first day working the makeover counter, and despite all the training, she felt completely unqualified to tell other people how to wear makeup, considering that she hardly ever wore any herself. Add to that the fact that she was still beyond distracted by her earlier conversation with Tia, and she was downright dangerous with an eyeliner pencil in her hand. Regardless, when Maria had dropped in the store to visit, Elizabeth jumped at the chance to do her makeup. She could practice without the risk of messing up on a real customer, plus it gave them some time to talk while Elizabeth was legitimately working.

"Okay." Maria groaned, crossing one leg over the other. "I just love being a guinea pig."

"It's only makeup," Elizabeth assured her, bending down and carefully blending the blush into Maria's cheeks the way she'd been taught. "It does wash off."

"Thank God," Maria whispered, which Elizabeth chose to ignore.

Finishing with the blush, Elizabeth turned around to search for some eyeliner in the clear plastic cosmetics bin. She selected the brown pencil instead of the black one, thinking it would bring out the flecks of lightness in Maria's dark eyes. She bent down a little to apply the eyeliner just underneath Maria's left eye, but when she took off the pencil's gold cap, she realized that she had somehow mistakenly pulled out a silver-colored liner.

"Damn," she muttered, fumbling for the brown pencil she wanted. "Who wears silver anyway?"

"Liz?" Maria asked as Elizabeth finally found the espresso brown shade. "Is everything okay?"

Elizabeth's arms dropped. "Yes," she said automatically. "I mean, no," she amended. "I don't know." She listlessly lifted her hand to start on Maria's eye.

Once again Maria pulled back. "Whoa. Hold up. You wanna tell me what's wrong before you put that thing any closer to my eye?"

Elizabeth sighed. With one elbow she leaned on the top of the high pink counter, placing her other hand on her hip. Elizabeth had already briefed Maria on last night's scene when she'd seen her in school today, but she hadn't gone into the gory details of how her unfounded jealousy was driving her crazy. *Yet.* "I just keep thinking about Conner and Tia," she admitted, then stood up straight when she saw Carolee give her the evil eye at her unprofessional stance.

"Uh-huh," Maria said, adjusting the neckline on her boat-neck top so that her bra strap didn't show. "But I thought we decided that Conner and Tia are best friends, like you and me, so they must have *some* private conversations."

"That's the thing," Elizabeth said. She picked up the eyeliner again and began to apply it to Maria's eye before she could object. Elizabeth could feel Carolee's eyes on her, and she knew she had to at least *look* like she was working. "It's *not* the same. You and I are both girls. Conner and Tia aren't." She was silent for a moment as she concentrated on making a perfect straight line underneath Maria's eye. When she was finished, she took a step back and assessed her work, then bent to do the other eye. "I mean, they *do* touch each other a lot," she went on, squinting as she began to draw another line with the eye pencil. "They sometimes even kiss each other on the cheek. What's *that* about?"

In a sudden fit of anger Elizabeth lost her concentration and slipped, causing her to dip the eyeliner down and draw a jagged line almost to Maria's cheek. "Oh, sorry!" she said, fumbling to grab a damp sponge and wipe off the misplaced makeup.

"That's it," Maria announced, standing up and

walking over to the oval mirror that sat on the counter. "I'll do it myself." She grabbed the brown eyeliner out of Elizabeth's hands.

God. I am so pathetic. Elizabeth dropped down onto the stool that Maria had been sitting on. "I guess I'm really out of it," she mumbled. She looked down at her hands, fidgeting with the damp sponge. "And I do know that they're not necessarily attracted to each other."

"Good," Maria said, her back to Elizabeth as she continued to apply her makeup.

Elizabeth didn't feel any better, though. She moved to the edge of the stool. "But why did he talk to Tia about everything instead of me?" she asked. "Okay, so I was busy last night, but I still wanted to talk to him. He clammed up the minute I got to Tia's. And they made me feel like I was ruining the moment or something."

"You know what I think, Liz?" Maria turned around, the eyeliner now perfectly applied to both of her eyes.

"What?" Elizabeth asked.

"I think you should just talk to the guy and let him know how you're feeling," she suggested. "He is, after all, your boyfriend."

Elizabeth nodded as she slid off the stool. She knew Maria was right, but it was easier said than done. What would she say? *I'm jealous of Tia?* Conner would definitely laugh at her or at least think she was nuts.

"Is everything going all right over here?" Carolee's shrill voice suddenly rang out.

Elizabeth paled. Carolee had probably seen her slacking off. She knew she was just one horrible makeover away from getting fired.

"Oh, yes," Maria responded immediately, baring a fake but enormous smile. "I was getting a lesson in how to apply my makeup myself so that I can do it at home."

"How lovely!" Carolee beamed, giving Elizabeth an exaggerated wink. "What a wonderful idea, Elizabeth." Then she walked off, her beige heels clicking against the faux-marble floor.

Elizabeth let out a sigh of relief. "I owe you one," she told Maria as she watched her manager stroll around the store.

"Well, just do yourself a favor instead," Maria said. She lifted her little straw bag off the counter and pulled it onto her shoulder.

"What's that?" Elizabeth asked.

Maria grabbed onto both of Elizabeth's shoulders and stared into her eyes. "Talk to him."

"You've done a great job," Mrs. Sandborn told Conner as he dried off the last pot with the dishrag. "Now please, go. Have fun."

Conner nodded, putting down the rag and pot and wiping his damp hands on his jeans. The crazy thing was, he wouldn't have actually minded sticking around and hanging out with his mom and Megan a little longer. Dinner hadn't been half as bad as Conner had thought it would be. In all honesty, he'd sort of enjoyed himself. He felt more relaxed than he had in months.

Still, there was no reason to push it or anything.

"Yeah," he said, taking a step back. "Okay." He caught Megan's eye as she placed the cover on a Tupperware box. The girl was totally glowing. And this time, unlike when she'd been psyched about her father, Conner could kind of get where she was coming from. Because it seemed like it was actually possible that rehab had put their mom on track.

His mother let out a deep breath, pushing a strand of hair away from her face as she opened the overhead cabinet to stow the pots away. Every now and then throughout the night she'd lapsed into these shaky moments, where she looked a little uncertain, nervous. But at least she was actually there, in body *and* in mind, unlike the space-cadet-like state she always used to be in when she was drunk.

"See you guys later," he said, lifting his chin at his mom and walking out.

He bolted up the stairs, realizing that he was actually smiling from tonight's family dinner. Now, that was a definite first.

He headed into his room, psyched to call Elizabeth and tell her about everything that had gone on. Usually, when it came to his family, Conner was the last person who wanted to spill. But for once he wanted to talk about it. And he wanted to talk about it with Elizabeth. Maybe they could go for a drive.

He picked up the cordless and dialed, leaning on the edge of his desk.

"Hello," Elizabeth's mom answered after two rings.

"Mrs. Wakefield, hi," Conner said, trying hard to use his best parental voice. "Could I speak to Liz?"

"Actually, she's still at work," Mrs. Wakefield told him.

Still at work? Conner glanced at his digital alarm clock. Did the girl ever come home? "Oh, okay," he said. *So much for sharing the good news,* he thought, deflated.

"Should I leave her a message?" Mrs. Wakefield asked.

Conner sighed. "Yeah. Just tell her I called. Thanks." He clicked off the phone and tossed it onto his bed.

He couldn't remember the last time that Elizabeth was actually there when he'd called.

"It was so surreal," Conner told Tia a couple of hours later at House of Java. "She was almost like another person."

Tia's eyes widened. She was totally absorbed by everything Conner was saying. She was totally absorbed by *Conner* and the completely uncharacteristically psyched state he was in. His green eyes were practically dancing, and there was even sort of a smile on his lips—or a smile by Conner's standards.

And when he'd called her a little while earlier, he'd said that he really wanted to hang out and talk. The Conner that Tia knew never *really* wanted to talk. At least, he'd never admit it if he did.

House of Java was packed tonight, so the two of them were stuffed into a green minisofa near the entrance, and Tia was sitting so close to him that she could basically feel all the happy vibes shooting directly from his body. *Talk about being like another person,* Tia thought, lifting her legs onto the couch and hugging them. His excitement was contagious.

"So, what *was* she like?" she asked before reaching for her mug of decaf latte.

Conner settled into the corner of the couch, draping his arm across the back, behind Tia's head. "Well, I mean, she was kinda tense and shaky at times," he explained. "But she was also one hundred percent *there.* She listened when Megan was talking, she was funny, she drank *water.* . . ." Conner drifted off for a moment, his eyes losing their sharp focus. Then he shook his head and stared right back at Tia. "I haven't seen her like that for years, Tee."

"Wow," she said, placing a hand on his knee. "That's amazing."

"I know." Conner's leg started to bounce up and down. "Tell me about it."

God, he was so cute like this! So completely un-Conner, yet still him in a way—just a more light-hearted version. He looked like a little boy. Tia leaned forward and gave him a big hug. "I'm so

80

happy for you," she told him, pulling away.

But as she did, something a little bit strange happened. Tia had hugged Conner a million times before and never thought twice about it, but tonight, well, she felt something. Not a big something, just an itty-bitty something, but the fact that she felt anything at all—the fact that she noted the feel of Conner's unshaved cheek and his soapy, masculine smell—was enough to weird her out. And now, as they smiled at each other, she could swear that she felt some sort of supercharged energy between them. A more than platonic energy. Feeling uncomfortable, she quickly glanced away, reaching for her mug of latte.

"Yeah," Conner told her. "I guess I am too."

Tia looked back at him as she sipped her coffee, and her weird feeling disappeared instantly. This was *Conner*. Of course only platonic energy flowed between them. *His upbeat mood is just throwing me off*, she told herself, putting her coffee back down on the little black table in front of them.

Relaxing, she pulled her green elastic out of her ponytail, letting her long, dark hair fall against her shoulders.

"See?" she said, nudging Conner playfully. "Sometimes good things do happen."

"Yeah," Conner answered. A strand of Tia's hair had fallen in front of her eyes, and Conner pushed it away with his finger. Tia did her best to ignore the very nonplatonic feeling *that* action caused. "Let's just hope it lasts," he added.

81

Tia couldn't help getting caught up in the moment as she stared back at him. It felt intense to momentarily view her best friend in a new light.

"Yeah," she whispered, almost forgetting what they were talking about. Then she snapped to and remembered. His mother. This was important. "You know what?" she said. "I think it *will* last."

Then she stood up to go to the bathroom and splash some cold water on her face. And pull herself out of this *Twilight Zone* moment and into the real world, where Conner was her best friend.

And *just* her best friend.

Maria Slater

I know it's a total cliché, but honesty really is the best policy.

When I was with Conner, everyone kept things from me because they wanted to spare my feelings. Things like the fact that Liz and Conner were falling for each other behind my back. As if _that_ were a smart tidbit to keep secret. Isn't it funny how people think they're doing the right thing when it's really the worst move possible?

Well, I'm not going to do that. Liz has concerns about Conner and Tia. And whether they're justified or not, she should make them known. I'm sure Liz is wrong about there being anything between them, but she'd feel so much better if she just let them both know how she felt.

I'm all about being up-front. It's better to get things out in the open than to have them fester inside until you finally explode.

But I know Liz. She doesn't think that way.

She won't say a word. She'll keep everything to herself.

That's where I come in.

Trust me. Liz'll thank me one day.

CHAPTER
A Mood You Don't Want to Mess With

"I'm glad you needed a ride," Elizabeth told Maria as she pulled her Jeep to a stop at a red light. "I'm not in the mood to be alone."

What a total understatement, she thought, pressing on the gas pedal as the light turned green. The truth was, whenever she had a moment to herself, she was tortured with thoughts of Conner and Tia. Thoughts that she knew were ridiculous. So, when Maria had said that her mom had dropped her off at the mall and that she'd stick around and wait for Elizabeth's shift to be over to catch a ride, Elizabeth was more than relieved to have the distraction of Maria's company.

"Yeah. I feel like hanging out too," Maria said, moving the passenger seat back to accommodate her extra-long legs. "Hey. You want to go to House of Java and chill for a little while?"

Elizabeth lifted her eyebrows, considering this. "Sure. Why not? I already did all my homework in study hall." She glanced behind her and quickly moved into the right lane so that she could make the turn toward House of Java. "I'll call Conner when we get there," she added, thinking aloud. "Maybe he'll want to join us."

"Cool." Maria pulled a tiny round mirror out of her straw bag and examined her reflection. "You know, I have to say, for someone who hardly wears makeup, I did a damn good job on myself."

Elizabeth rolled her eyes as she pulled into House of Java's packed parking lot. "Wonderful. Maybe you can take over my job when they fire me."

"They are *not* going to fire you," Maria protested. "Oh, there's a spot," she said, pointing to the left, where a white Cabriolet was pulling out. Elizabeth drove over and put on her blinker. "You just can't do makeovers when you're worried about Conner, that's all," Maria added.

"You're right." Elizabeth drove into the space. "But I'm not going to worry about Conner anymore anyway. I know it's all in my head."

Maria nodded. "Good," she said, opening her door.

Elizabeth sighed as she turned off the ignition. She could say she wasn't going to obsess about Conner and Tia, but she also knew that she couldn't help the nagging thoughts from crowding her brain space.

"Hey, Liz, I'm gonna go in there for a second and get a pack of gum," Maria said, pointing to the Valley Hills Convenience Store, adjacent to the House of Java. "You want anything?"

"No, thanks," Elizabeth responded as she locked the car. "I'll meet you inside."

"Okay." Maria headed over to the store's glass-doored entrance.

Elizabeth walked around the parking lot to the front of HOJ. *This is just what I need,* she thought as she pushed open the door. *I'll call Conner and have some downtime with him, and my head will be clear again.*

But as soon as she took one step inside the aromatic coffee shop, she froze in the doorway.

Conner was already there. With Tia.

They were sitting on the green love seat a couple of feet ahead. Elizabeth swallowed. The *love seat.* Their backs were to Elizabeth, but she recognized their profiles immediately. Normally she'd just run up and say hi, but seeing them there like that, given all her recent worries, she just couldn't. Her stomach turned over, and her legs felt rooted into the floor.

Was it just her imagination, or were they gazing at each other in an intense way? A majorly intense way . . .

Elizabeth paled. She felt like she was going to throw up. And just when she thought she couldn't take anymore, she saw Conner lift his hand and tenderly push a strand of Tia's dark hair away from her face.

Oh my God. Without even thinking, Elizabeth turned around and bolted out of there on weak legs. Everything was a blur as she headed back to her car.

All she knew was that she had to get out of there, and go home, and cry.

"Liz!" Maria called, walking out of the convenience store. "Where are you going? What's wrong?"

Shaking her head, Elizabeth searched frantically in her black purse for her car keys. "He was there," she told Maria, still trying to process what she'd seen.

"Who?" Maria asked, running up right next to her.

Pulling out her keys, Elizabeth let out a shaky sigh and looked at Maria. "Conner," she whispered, glancing around to make sure he hadn't come outside. "And Tia. They were there together."

"Okay." Maria crossed her arms over her chest. "And that's a problem because?"

"*Because*," Elizabeth hissed, her patience at the moment being way less than tissue thin. "It was just the two of them there."

Maria's eyes opened wider. "And?"

"*And* they looked very . . . close," she said, her cheeks heating up as she realized how stupid she sounded. But still, she knew what she saw. "And Conner touched her hair. In this very . . . intimate way."

Maria threw her hands up in the air. "All right," she said. "I give up. You have totally let your imagination drive you to the point of insanity."

"Maria!" Elizabeth said, enraged. She couldn't believe that now she had to put up with Maria calling her crazy. "I know what I saw!"

"You were in there for all of two seconds," Maria pointed out. "Don't you think you could've *misinterpreted* whatever it was that you saw? And do you think that if they *were* having an affair, or whatever, they'd go there where everyone could see them?"

Huh. Elizabeth blinked. She bit her lip. Maria did have a point there. "Well, uh . . ."

"And," Maria continued, "you were at work, so it's completely normal that Conner would hang out with Tia instead. Not to mention that they *are* best friends. And not to mention that there could have been other people with them that you didn't even notice."

Elizabeth looked down at the asphalt, her cheeks flaming up. *She's right,* she thought, feeling beyond lame. Why had she jumped to such ridiculous conclusions? God, since when did she get so paranoid? Elizabeth cringed as she thought about how she'd run out of there like a maniac instead of just saying hi to her boyfriend and close friend like a normal person would.

"Liz?" Maria asked gently, touching her shoulder. "You okay?"

Elizabeth looked back up and nodded. She fidgeted with her keys. "I don't know what's gotten into me," she confessed quietly.

Maria gave her a quick hug. "Jealousy," she told her. "*That's* why you have to talk to Conner. Make him more sensitive to your feelings. Otherwise you're gonna end up making *yourself* nuts. For no reason."

"I know," Elizabeth agreed. Her stomach was tied into knots from her rapidly changing emotions, and she could barely make eye contact with Maria. She hated feeling so weak. It was humiliating.

"So," Maria said, cocking her head in the direction of House of Java. "You wanna go in?"

Elizabeth kicked at the ground with her sandal-clad foot. "I don't think so." She was exhausted and worked up, and she knew that she couldn't be around Conner and Tia without them wondering what was wrong with her. Admitting her delusional jealousies to Maria was one thing, but telling Conner and Tia was something else entirely. Something she wasn't prepared to do. "I'm tired. Let's just go home."

"Okay," Maria said, sounding concerned. She hooked her arm through Elizabeth's. "But you will talk to him, right?"

Elizabeth shook her head as they walked over to her car. Then she just sighed again and said, "Maybe."

"No cheerleading today," Jessica said to Tia as they walked out of the theater after drama class on Wednesday afternoon. "What are you going to do?"

Tia hugged her green-and-white messenger bag to her body and grinned. Coach had canceled today's cheerleading practice the day before, explaining that since it was so late in the season, they didn't need to meet every single afternoon anymore. Tia was more than grateful. She could use the break. "Absolutely nothing," she responded blissfully.

"Me too." Jessica smiled, pulling on her thin, fitted denim jacket. "Well, see you later. I'm gonna try to catch up with Liz," she said, starting down the hall.

"Later," Tia called after her. She turned to walk in the other direction, toward her locker.

"Tia? Could you hold up a sec?" Maria asked, jogging up from behind her.

Tia stopped in place. "Sure. What's up?"

Maria glanced down at her hands, then walked away from the rush of students streaming down the hallway. Tia followed her, concerned. By the looks of Maria's expression, this seemed like something heavy.

"It's about Liz," Maria explained, leaning against locker 79.

"Liz?" Tia dropped her bag to the floor, straddling it between her feet. "What's wrong with Liz?"

"Oh, it's nothing major," Maria assured her quickly. She put her hands in the back pockets of her baggy jeans and stared down at her sneakers. "It's just that, well, lately she's been kinda insecure about you and Conner."

Tia blinked. *Huh?* "What about me and Conner?"

Maria chewed on the inside of her lip. "Well, you guys spend a lot of time together, and she's starting to wonder if there's something between you two."

Tia blinked again, completely confused. "What?" Her large brown eyes opened even larger than their normal size. She couldn't believe her ears. But then, suddenly remembering the weird vibes that she'd experienced with Conner last night, her face heated up. "What do you mean?" she added, crossing her arms over her bare stomach, where her white cropped top ended. "That's insane."

Maria raised her eyes back up to Tia's face. "I know," she said, playing with her silver bracelet. "That's why I'm telling you. I wasn't sure that I should get involved, but Liz would never say anything herself, and I wanted to clear things up before things got tense."

"Tense?" Tia repeated, her mouth dropping open. "Just what exactly does Liz think is going on?"

"Oh, nothing necessarily," Maria told her. "It's not like she thinks you guys are fooling around or anything," she explained, and again Tia's face felt extremely hot. "It's just that she knows that Conner's been talking to you about his mom and stuff, and he hasn't been talking to her at all, so she's starting to wonder . . ."

Maria's voice trailed off, and now it was Tia's turn to look down at the floor. All of a sudden she felt really bad. She knew Elizabeth was supersensitive, and Tia hated to think that *she* was the source of Elizabeth's anxiety. The fact that she'd been just the slightest bit attracted to Conner last night didn't make her feel any better either. Sighing, she sank to the ground, leaning against the locker. Maria sat down next to her.

"I just think Conner needs someone to talk to right now," Tia explained, looking down and drawing an imaginary design on her cargo pant leg. "And Liz has been so busy, so he's been coming to me."

"That's what I figured." Maria stretched her legs out in front of her and nearly tripped a curly-haired freshman guy. She brought her legs back up. "And that makes total sense. I mean, I know that you and Conner are best friends. It's ridiculous to think that anything would ever happen between you two."

"Right," Tia said, staring down at her Skechers and willing all of her uncool thoughts from last night to disappear. "Exactly."

"But since Liz is in love with Conner, her sense of reality is a little clouded," Maria went on. "I'm kind of worried that she's going to get herself all upset and angry for no reason. All she needs is a little reassurance, though. And for Conner to confide in *her*."

Tia lifted her head and looked at Maria, not knowing what to think of all this. All she knew was that she felt guilty. For what, she wasn't quite sure. After all, Elizabeth didn't know about Tia's brief nonplatonic thoughts concerning Conner. And that's all they were: brief and just thoughts.

"So I was wondering," Maria continued. "Maybe you could talk to Conner about it." Tia lifted her eyebrows in surprise. "I'd do it myself," Maria quickly added, "but I'm not at all close with him."

Tia stretched her arms out in front of her, thinking. This was definitely a bizarre situation, and talking to Conner would be no picnic. But Tia definitely liked Elizabeth too much to have her be upset with her, regardless of whether she had the right to be or not.

"Sure." Tia shrugged. "Whatever. I'll talk to him."

Maria broke into a huge smile, causing Tia to wonder exactly why Maria was so invested in all of this. And why Elizabeth couldn't have spoken to her herself. "Great," Maria said. "Thanks."

"Yeah," Tia responded warily. She suddenly felt really unsure about what she'd agreed to do. Or at least *why* she was doing it. "No problem."

Maria glanced at her watch and got to her feet, standing up. "Gotta go," she said. "Thanks again, Tee."

Tia just nodded and waved as Maria bounced off into the crowd. She hugged her knees to her chest and stared out at the sea of legs before her. She sat there like that for a couple of minutes, trying to process the conversation she'd just had. And after a moment she felt sort of annoyed.

Sure, Liz is Conner's girlfriend, she thought, *but Conner's always come to me, regardless of who he's going out with. And no one's ever interfered in our relationship before.*

Then she realized that she was being stupid. Conner had never had a real girlfriend before, just girls he was hooking up with. Tia knew that Elizabeth was a lot more important to him than that. Elizabeth was a lot more important to *Tia* than that.

And, Tia thought, standing up, *if I were in Liz's shoes, I'd want him to come to me too. If Angel had confided in someone else while we were together, I would've been crazy jealous.*

She lifted her bag up off the floor and pulled it onto her shoulder. Walking into the throng of students, she realized one more thing.

She wasn't going to talk to Conner about Elizabeth. Maria might feel comfortable getting involved in Conner and Elizabeth's relationship, but Tia sure didn't. The only thing she could do was back off.

"Andy! Could you stop doing that? It's completely annoying!"

Andy caught the red plastic ball that he'd been throwing up at his ceiling for the past few minutes and held on to it. It took great restraint not to toss it up again, but he could tell that Tia was in a mood. A mood you did not want to mess with. Not if you valued your life.

He and Tia had been hanging out in his room for the past half hour or so. Tia had come over after school, saying she wanted to have a fun, brain-free session with him. Well, so far their hanging out might have been brain-free, but Andy wouldn't have quite described it as fun. Tia had been in the same position ever since she'd arrived: cross-legged, leaning against his gray platform bed, and watching TV. The thing was, Andy could tell that she wasn't really *watching* the talk show that was on at the moment. She was looking at it, but from her dazed expression and dulled eyes, it was clear that her mind was elsewhere.

She's probably just missing Angel, Andy thought, sitting up on the edge of his bed.

"Sorry, Tee. I'll stop," Andy said. He stood up and walked over to his desk in the corner of the room, putting the ball down on top of it next to his cluttered mess of notebooks and pens. As he stuck a blue Bic in his mouth, chewing on the end, he realized that he was having a severe fidgeting problem. In fact, ever since his date last weekend with Six, he'd been a fidgeting machine. He knew it was because he couldn't stop thinking about what had gone down with her. Or, more appropriately, what *hadn't* gone down with her.

Andy turned around and hopped onto his desk. He took the pen out of his mouth and began to scribble on a yellow Post-it pad, looking over at Tia. It crossed his mind that given Tia's obviously crappy mood, this might not be the best time to talk to her about relationships. He ran a hand through his red hair and tried to hold in his thoughts, but it was useless. He was going nuts thinking about Six.

"Hey, Tee?" he asked, still scribbling away.

Tia silently turned away from the television set and looked at him, raising her eyebrows.

He put the pen and pad down, rubbing both hands on his beat-up old corduroys. "Uh, how do you know if you're attracted to someone?"

Tia smirked and rolled her eyes. She actually *smirked.* Picking up the pen and pad, he began to nervously doodle again.

"You just *know*," Tia told him. "It's not the kind of thing you need to think about."

Andy nodded as he looked down at the little yellow piece of paper. He felt too embarrassed to speak.

Then, out of the corner of his eye, he saw Tia tilt her head. She turned all the way around so that she was facing him. "Why?" she asked him, staring at him now. "Are you not attracted to Six?"

Andy began to doodle harder, almost poking holes in the paper with his pen. He shrugged. "I don't know," he mumbled. "I mean, well . . . I guess . . . I definitely think she's hot."

Tia stood and walked over to him, taking the pen and paper out of his hand and putting them down. She pulled herself onto the desk so that she was sitting next to him, her short legs dangling above the carpeted floor.

"Andy, it shouldn't be that hard to figure out," she told him.

Great, Andy thought. So he definitely was a freak. He finally had a girlfriend—a beautiful girlfriend— but he wasn't into her. What was his deal?

"When you're attracted to someone, it feels very strong," she went on, this time in a gentler tone of voice. Andy finally glanced at her, and she looked back at him with sympathetic eyes. "You'll know it when you feel it, Andy," she promised, lightly placing a hand on his arm.

Man, I hope so, he thought.

"And you know what else?" Tia asked, then went

97

on without waiting for Andy to respond. "Life would be a lot easier if those hormones *weren't* so strong." She broke her gaze from Andy and looked down at her hands. She picked up his pad of paper again, ripping off the sheet he'd been drawing on and crumpling it into a little ball. "Sometimes you're attracted to people you really don't want to be attracted to."

Tia uttered those last words with such gravity that Andy forgot all about his own problems with Six and focused on Tia. Her big brown eyes almost looked watery, and she was gripping on to that crumpled-up wad of paper for dear life.

She must be totally regretting hooking up with Trent Maynor, he realized as he watched her.

Shaking his head, he pulled at the collar of his T-shirt and slid off the desk. *If this is what relationships do to you, I'm ready to get out.*

Really. Who needed this?

"You are so dead!" Maria exclaimed, stealing the basketball from Ken and dribbling it up to the net in his driveway.

Catching his breath, Ken stood back, leaning forward with his hands on his knees. He smiled as Maria went for the layup. He knew she would get it. She was the layup queen.

Sure enough, Maria jumped up and took aim, and the ball easily swooshed through the basket.

"Nice one!" a woman's voice exclaimed before Ken had the chance to say so himself. He and Maria both turned around to see Asha walking up the driveway from her lime green Volkswagen Beetle, which she had parked at the curb.

"Oh, hey, Asha," Ken said, actually glad to see her. After his father had ditched out on dinner the other night, he wasn't quite sure what Asha's and his status was anymore. But the more Ken thought about it, the more he realized that it wouldn't be the worst thing if everything worked out for Asha and his father. Maybe she would even make Ken's father a happier person—just the way Maria did for Ken.

"Hi, guys," she said. She took off her cream-colored fitted suit jacket as she neared them, revealing a silk tank top underneath. "Maria, since you haven't made any definite career plans yet, I wouldn't rule out the WNBA."

Maria laughed. Holding the basketball in her arms, she wiped the sweat off her forehead. "Yeah, right," she said. "I'm sure all the scouts will be knocking down my door."

"Hey, you never know," Asha responded. Her brown eyes twinkled with amusement.

"So, uh, what's up?" Ken asked. "Dad's not home, you know."

Asha nodded, and the black curls that were loose from her bun-type hairdo bounced around her sharp-angled face. "Yes, I do know. I just left him at work. He was going into a meeting, which is why I thought it might be a good time to talk to you."

Ken swallowed. She wasn't going to get mad at

him for the other night, was she? He already felt bad enough as it was. "Me?" Ken looked at Maria, and she shrugged. "What for?"

"Well, I wanted to get a little present for your father," Asha began, fiddling with her keys. "And I thought you would be the perfect person to help me."

Ken raised his eyebrows in surprise. A gift? This was interesting. "Um, okay. What do you need?"

Asha bit her lip. "Information, basically. Your father once mentioned that there was some football award that he wanted to get reframed. I just can't remember which one it was. Or where it is."

Ken's eyes lit up. He was impressed. And he knew exactly the award she was referring to. It was from his father's college days, and he treasured it, but the glass part of its frame was cracked. "His junior-year MVP award," Ken told her. "It's in his study. I can get it for you." He ran a hand through his blond hair, the residual guilt that he still felt from the other night giving him another sudden idea. "You know, there's one store that my dad always goes to for framing. I'll go with you if you want."

"Really?" Asha's face brightened. "That would be great. Thanks."

"No problem," Ken said. He was completely impressed that Asha was making this big effort for his father. The least he could do was help her out a little.

Asha glanced at her watch. "I've got to run to make an appointment in a few minutes. But how about tomorrow evening, around six? Could you go with me then?"

"Sure," Ken said. "Okay."

"Wonderful. Bye, Maria," she said, giving a little wave. "Start practicing your free throws. Ken, I'll see you tomorrow."

"Bye," Maria said with a laugh as Asha hurried down the driveway and got into her car. "I'm proud of you," she told Ken, giving him a peck on his cheek. "That was very nice."

Ken shrugged. "What can I say? I'm a nice guy." He quickly grabbed the basketball out of Maria's hands, dribbling it and running up to the net. Setting himself up, he made his shot . . . and missed.

"Yeah," Maria teased, standing behind him. "Just maybe not the best basketball player."

TIA RAMIREZ

~~DEAR ANGEL:~~

HI, ~~SWEETIE.~~ WHAT'S UP? IT'S
SORT OF STRANGE TO WRITE YOU A
LETTER, BUT A PHONE CALL SEEMED
~~MORE THAN I COULD HANDLE~~ LIKE A
LITTLE TOO MUCH, AND AN E-MAIL
SEEMED A LITTLE TOO CASUAL.

NOT THAT I HAVE THAT MUCH TO
SAY OR ANYTHING. WELL, OF COURSE,
I HAVE PLENTY TO SAY. AFTER ALL, WE
HAVEN'T SPOKEN IN A WHILE—
I HAVE TONS OF STORIES FOR YOU.
BUT I GUESS I'M NOT SUPPOSED TO
SHARE THEM WITH YOU ANYMORE. OR
SOMETHING. RIGHT?

SO I GUESS ALL I WANT TO SAY
IS ~~I LOVE YOU. I MISS YOU. I'M~~
~~THINKING ABOUT YOU.~~ HI.

FORGET IT. IT'S EASIER NOT TO TRY
TO COMMUNICATE WITH HIM AT ALL.

Ken Matthews

<u>List</u> <u>of</u> <u>places</u> <u>to</u> <u>take</u> <u>Asha</u> <u>to</u> <u>tomorrow:</u>

   Valley Frames on Palm Lane
   Corner Market: pick up six-pack of
Bull's Horn Lager (Dad's favorite
microbrewery)
   Sunflower Bakery: get Dad's favorite
espresso brownies
   Blockbuster Video: rent <u>Road</u> <u>Warrior,</u>
Dad's favorite movie

CHAPTER 7
Coming Up Empty

Elizabeth lay nestled under her burgundy covers on Thursday morning, debating whether or not to play sick and stay home from school. She hadn't done that in years, and she felt childish even considering it, but she couldn't help it. Besides, the way her head was throbbing and her body was aching, she might as well be sick.

She'd barely even seen Conner at school, except for some rushed moments during lunch and with everyone else around. She'd worked again last night, and they'd only spoken when she'd come home and called him. Their conversation had been painfully brief. It was just killing Elizabeth that Conner hadn't told her much about what was happening with his mom. She knew things were going better than expected, but she didn't know the details.

And she was sure Tia did.

Elizabeth sat up, hugging her pillow. She was not going to let her jealousy eat away at her. Especially when Maria was right. She had no reason to be jealous in the first place.

Jessica suddenly burst into the room, wearing only two pink fluffy towels, one around her body and one wrapped around her hair. She headed straight for Elizabeth's closet but did a double take when she saw Elizabeth sitting in bed.

"Uh, Liz?" she said, holding her towel up with one hand. "Are you planning to go to school today or what?"

Elizabeth groaned as she pulled her legs out from under the covers. "I guess."

"Well, you better get moving," Jessica told her, disappearing inside the closet.

Elizabeth dropped her feet to the plush carpeted floor and sighed. Her sister's energy was a little too much for her this morning. Jessica reemerged from the closet, a pair of Elizabeth's dark jeans in her arms, and took a long look at Elizabeth, her eyebrows furrowing and her forehead wrinkling.

"Is something wrong?" she asked. She walked over and sat down next to Elizabeth on the bed.

Elizabeth looked down, gathering the bunched-up cotton sheets in her hands. She hadn't seen that much of her sister lately, what with Elizabeth working at Sedona and Jessica always either at cheerleading practice or working at House of Java, so she hadn't had a chance to tell her what was going on. And she didn't feel like getting into it now. "No. I'm just tired."

"Come on, Liz." Jessica took the towel off her head, letting her damp blond hair fall against her shoulders. "You don't sleep late unless something's bothering you. What's up?"

Elizabeth stood and took a couple of heavy steps toward her dresser. She picked up her brush and attempted to untangle her knotty morning hair. "Nothing," she said. But when she glanced back at Jessica, her sister gave her a look that said, *Oh, please.*

Elizabeth regarded herself with half-closed eyes in the mirror above her dresser and saw that she was a total mess. A huge pimple (from emotional stress, no doubt) was forming on her chin, and she had bags under her red-rimmed eyes.

"Fine, there is something," she amended, realizing that it was useless to try to hide it. "But it's just a little thing."

"Okay," Jessica responded, walking up behind her. "So what is it?"

Elizabeth looked at Jessica's reflection in the mirror. "It's just that Conner and Tia have been spending a lot of time together lately," she explained, trying to sound as nonchalant as possible. "And I've barely seen Conner myself." She winced as the brush got caught in an especially bad knot. "But whatever. I know I have no right to be upset. I mean, they are best friends," she said, finally managing to get the brush through the huge tangle.

"But you're his girlfriend," Jessica pointed out.

Elizabeth's stomach tied into the same knotted state as her hair. She put down the brush and turned around to face her twin. "What are you saying?"

Jessica shrugged. "I'm saying that I think you do have a right to be upset."

Now Elizabeth's stomach dropped to the floor. This was not what she needed to hear. "You do?"

"Well, yeah." Jessica put Elizabeth's jeans down on the dresser and picked up the brush herself. She started to work on her hair, darting her eyes back and forth from Elizabeth to her own reflection. "I understand that Conner and Tia are friends and everything, but you should always come first. He shouldn't be spending time with Tia instead of you."

"But they've always hung out a lot," Elizabeth argued, suddenly feeling desperate to convince Jessica, even though she didn't really believe it herself. "I can't ask them to change that just because Conner and I are together now."

"Yes, you can." Jessica turned away from the mirror, looking at Elizabeth with wide eyes. "And Tia should respect Conner's and your relationship. I mean, let's say Evan started going out with someone—"

"That's totally different," Elizabeth interrupted, thankful to have something to object to. "You've known Evan for two weeks. Conner and Tia have been friends for years."

"So?" Jessica asked. She glanced at herself in the mirror, then, apparently approving of her hair, put down the brush. "Pretend that Evan and I have been friends for years too. Point is, I love hanging out with Evan. But if he had a girlfriend, I'd back off, no problem."

"It's still different," Elizabeth protested, her head now pounding like crazy. This discussion was only making her feel worse. She did not want to be jealous, and she did not want to be mad at Tia. Trying to force these thoughts out of her brain, she opened up the top dresser drawer and pulled out a bra and a pair of underpants.

"Fine. Think of it this way," Jessica went on mercilessly. "Maria's your best friend, right?"

"Yes," Elizabeth mumbled. She opened the middle drawer and grabbed the first T-shirt she saw.

"But as much as you love her, is it more important for you to spend time with her? Or with Conner?"

As Elizabeth closed the dresser drawer, she looked up at her sister, her brain hopelessly searching for an argument, something to prove Jessica wrong. Something to show that Conner *didn't* care more about Tia than he cared about her. But she came up empty.

Which matched how her heart suddenly felt. Empty.

Conner cut the engine and turned off his Mustang's headlights. As he stepped out of his car, locking it and then heading for his front door, he was feeling pretty upbeat. He'd just had a good time hanging out with Andy (the poor dude was so confused), and even though Elizabeth had to do her usual lipstick pushing after school, she'd told him that her shift ended early tonight and she really wanted to see him later. Which was cool with Conner. He was looking forward to finally getting some quality time with her.

Add to that the fact that Conner wasn't worried about his mother anymore, and Conner's spirits felt lighter than they had in months.

He opened the front door and walked into his house, the smell of tomato sauce immediately filling his nostrils. *Maybe in years,* he corrected.

"Conner, where have you been?" Mrs. Sandborn asked, walking out of the kitchen and wiping her hands on a striped dishrag. "You missed dinner."

Conner shrugged. It wasn't like there had ever been a designated dinnertime in this household before. "I didn't know we were eating together. I grabbed some pizza."

Conner's mom shook her head. She adjusted the backing of her diamond-stud earring. "Well, next time call me if you're going to be late and ask if it's all right."

"What?" Conner said, narrowing his eyes.

"You can't just come and go as you please anymore," she said. Her blue eyes were gentle, but her voice sounded unusually strict. "You need to keep me informed of your whereabouts."

Conner could barely find his voice. He had taken care of himself—and Megan—for years, and suddenly she was stepping in to be in charge?

"Mom, you can't just waltz back in here and change the rules," he told her, feeling anger rise inside him. Where did she get off?

His mother sighed. She looked down at the ground, then back up at Conner. "That's just the problem," she said in a quiet voice. "There have never been any rules here. And I know it's my fault, but that's going to change. Starting now."

This was just perfect. His mother had finally decided to become a parent when Conner no longer needed one. And after years of dealing on his own, he wasn't about to start asking his mommy for permission for anything. He kicked at the unstained wooden floor with his work boot.

"You got one thing right," he muttered. "It *is* your fault. And that's your problem, not mine."

Then he turned and stalked up the stairs, without giving his mother a second glance.

Somehow he knew he'd feel horrible if he did.

"I guess I don't really need to ask this, given the Ed Matthews tour you've taken me on this evening," Asha teased as she and Ken walked down one of Blockbuster Video's superlong, superfreezing aisles. They had already dropped off his father's award at the framing store, and it was going to be ready to pick up in half an hour. Meanwhile they had also hit the bakery and the market and were now making their final rounds at the video store. "But are you okay with me dating your father? Does it bother you at all?"

Ken stuffed his hands into his jeans pockets. "No," he said finally. "Not really." He slowed his walk as they reached the *R* section of the action movies. "I'm not delusional or anything," he explained as he checked out the titles. "I'm not one of those kids who dreams of his parents getting back together. I wouldn't *want* them to. They fought like crazy." Ken felt his cheeks flame up at this admission. It might be true, but was that the best piece of information to give his dad's girlfriend?

"Mmmm." Asha crouched down as she scanned the video titles herself. "Same story with my parents. They argued so much, I couldn't wait for them to get a divorce," she said in a way that put Ken immediately at ease.

"Really?" he asked. "So did they?"

Asha picked up the box for *Ronin* and glanced at the summary on the back of it. "Yes. Thank God. It was the best thing they could've done. They're both so much happier now."

Ken nodded. "That's all I want. I just want Dad to be happy."

Asha placed the box back on the shelf and smiled, nudging Ken playfully. "You know what? You're a model son."

"Not really." Ken shook his head and shifted his weight from one foot to the other. The truth was, Ken wanted his father and Asha's relationship to work out for selfish reasons more than out of any concern for his father. Mainly because his dad might chill out a little and be in an overall better mood if it did. Translation: He might be an easier person to live with.

"Here it is," she said, reaching out for the *Road Warrior* box. As she regarded the front of it, her long, classical-looking nose scrunched up. "Well, whether or not you're the model son, I am definitely the model girlfriend," she said. "Because watching this movie will take serious devotion."

"Hey," Ken protested, pointing at the video's box. "That's a classic."

Asha rolled her eyes. "Like father, like son," she teased. But she smiled and, *Road Warrior* in hand, strolled toward the checkout line.

Ken followed, grinning. And thinking that he could definitely deal with having Asha around more permanently.

Jessica Wakefield

To: ev-man@swiftnet.com
From: jess1@cal.rr.com
Subject: Yo

Evan:

How's it going? Didn't really see you in school today. Did you skip out on lunch?

Anyway. Wanted to see if you'd like to hang out tomorrow night. You know, a nondate. A friend thing. We could go to the Riot.

Let me know.

Jess

Evan Plummer

To: jess1@cal.rr.com
From: ev-man@swiftnet.com
Subject: You're on

   Sure. Sounds like fun. As long as
we're clear that it is not a date. I
don't want to be leading you on or
anything. :)

Jessica Wakefield

To: ev-man@swiftnet.com
From: jess1@cal.rr.com
Subject: We're clear

Evan:
   No worries. I don't want your body.
But maybe, just in case, we should
both invite other people to come. Just
to make sure it isn't a date in the
slightest. :)
   Later.
                    Jess

Evan Plummer

To: mcdermott@cal.rr.com,
marsden1@swiftnet.com,
mslater@swiftnet.com,
tee@swiftnet.com,
kenQB@swiftnet.com
From: ev-man@swiftnet.com
Subject: Be there

Tomorrow night. The Riot.
Everyone's going. Join in the fun.

CHAPTER
Rather Be Solving Calculus Problems

8

"Her giving orders is such a joke." Conner leaned back in Elizabeth's swiveling desk chair and ran a hand through his scruffy hair. "How can she seriously expect us to listen to her when she was nonexistent for years?"

Elizabeth nodded, hugging her legs to her chest as she sat on her bed. As bad as she felt for Conner, she also felt legitimately happy for the first time in days. Happy that Conner was confiding in *her*. Letting her in. *Thank God I made him come over tonight,* she thought, taking in his strained, square jaw muscles, his tense-looking eyes. She was extremely glad that she was the one he had come to. And not only that, but they had been talking for hours. Elizabeth felt closer to him than she had in a long time.

"That must be hard," she responded, fiddling with her anklet. She felt like she could almost relate to how he was feeling in the tiniest way since she'd had trouble readjusting to living with her parents' rules after moving back in with them postearthquake. Still, she knew it was nothing compared to what Conner had to go through.

She bit her lip. "But part of the reason she was never really there was because she was—" Elizabeth paused, looking down at her cotton-candy-colored toenails. It was rare for Conner to be this open about his feelings, and she didn't want to push him away by saying the wrong thing. "Because she was drinking, right?"

Conner picked up the blue plastic Slinky that Jessica had given Elizabeth as a joke gift and played with it. "Try all of the reason," he muttered.

"Right." Elizabeth pushed her hair behind her ears. "Well, so maybe now that she's not drinking, she needs to do things like make rules for you guys and stuff. I mean, it might be hard, but maybe she'll start being more responsible overall. . . . You know?"

Conner didn't respond, but Elizabeth could tell by the way his jaw was clenching and unclenching that he was thinking her words over.

She moved to the edge of the bed and dropped her feet to the floor so that she was sitting directly across from him. "I'm not saying that you should forget everything and do whatever she says, but the fact that she's not drinking is a huge change. So maybe other things are going to have to change too."

For a long moment Conner was silent, staring at the Slinky as if it held the answers to everything. Elizabeth held her breath, worried that he was going to lash out at her for pointing out his mother's side.

But when Conner did finally look at her, his eyes were gentle. Almost tired. He put the Slinky back on the desk. "Yeah," he said, slouching in the chair. "Maybe."

Elizabeth smiled in relief. She reached out and touched Conner's knee.

Conner squeezed her hand, holding on to it. Then his eyes darted over to her alarm clock on her mahogany night table. He sighed. "Man. I do *not* want to go home," he said, slowly standing up. "I wish we were still living in the same house."

A wave of warmth washed over Elizabeth. The kind of closeness that had just passed between them was exactly what she had been craving. She tugged on the soft hem of Conner's worn-in gray T-shirt. "My parents might let you crash here; downstairs, of course. You never know—"

"That's all right." Conner quickly turned away to grab his car keys off the desk.

Elizabeth hugged herself as she stared at his back. What guy wouldn't want to spend the night in his girlfriend's house with the possibility of sneaking around? She glanced down and started playing with the ruffled edge of her comforter.

"Liz, what's up?" Conner asked, crouching down in front of her. "Something wrong?"

Elizabeth opened her mouth to complain, then quickly closed it as she looked into his insanely green eyes. More than anything, she didn't want to part with him on bad terms.

She shook her head. "No. I was just thinking."

"Oh," Conner whispered, nodding and gazing at her in an extremely sexy way. Then he leaned in and gave her a long, lingering kiss.

Elizabeth's arms and neck tingled with goose bumps as he pulled away. Her body felt like Silly Putty. Any trace of frustration that she'd had with him quickly vanished. "I needed that," she told him.

Half of Conner's mouth lifted into a smile. "Yeah. I could tell." He stood up. "So. You want to hang out tomorrow night?" he asked. "Just the two of us?"

Elizabeth grinned. She needed *that* too. "Yes. Definitely. And definitely just the two of us."

"Deal." Conner bent down and kissed her one more time. "Later," he said, before walking out the door.

"Later," Elizabeth whispered, even though he was already gone.

But that didn't matter. All that mattered was that he'd been here.

Elizabeth fell back, lying down on her bed.

Thank God, she thought, closing her eyes. They were back on track.

Andy lay stomach down on his carpeted floor, staring at the calculus problem in his spiral notebook before him. Not solving. Not computing. Not thinking.

Just staring.

Okay, okay, focus. Fo-cus, Andy thought, sitting up and raising his hands to his short red hair.

Concentrate. You want to get into college, remember? A good college. He kept his eyes on the problem for a few more moments, but soon the numbers started to form into a hazy blur before him.

His brain went on another tangent altogether. *What's the point?* he wondered, picking at the carpeting. He'd already been a mediocre student for three years. Was it really going to make a difference if he suddenly did better this semester? What college was going to say, "Hey, this guy sucked for most of high school. But look at his first semester senior year. Let's take 'im!"?

Just as he was about write all of this off as useless, he remembered his college counselor's mumbo jumbo. He'd said that some schools were impressed by an improvement of grades over the course of high school. And how, even if he didn't get into a good school for next year, if he got good grades now, he had a better shot of being able to transfer into a good college his sophomore year.

Okay. Focus, Andy recited to himself once again. He glanced over at his desk. Maybe he'd do better if he tried to work over there? *Nah,* he thought, lying back down. *Too uncomfortable.*

Suddenly the phone rang, and Andy dove across his bed to reach for the cordless, picking up on the first ring. Any excuse to procrastinate was a good one for him.

"Hello?" he said as he sat up and caught his breath.

"Andy?" a female voice asked.

Six. Andy could recognize her high-pitched tone anywhere. And considering how much he'd been worrying about what was happening between them, you'd think he'd dread talking to her. But because of his current state of homework avoidance, he was psyched. Chatting with Six was a legitimate reason to put off calculus a little while longer.

"Hey, Six. What's up?"

"Not much," she responded. "I . . . just called to say hi."

Andy stood and walked over to his desk. "Well, hi," he said, and Six immediately laughed. He grinned as he picked up the red plastic ball that he'd been playing with yesterday. Six was definitely good for his ego. She was his best audience, no doubt. "What have you been up to?" he asked.

"Nothing, really. We just finished dinner. My dad and I made these awesome salmon tacos for everyone. I was just about to start my math homework."

Andy leaned against the desk, throwing the ball up against the ceiling and catching it. "Funny. I was just avoiding mine. Doing a damn good job of it too."

Six giggled again. "You should be proud."

Andy shrugged, tossing the ball up again. Man, this ball-ceiling game was addictive. *I should market it or something,* he thought. "Yeah, well, I try," he joked.

"You know, I saw you running out of school after the bell rang today. I called after you, but you didn't hear," Six told him.

"Oh. Sorry about that."

"That's okay. I know you didn't mean it," she said, just as Andy threw the ball up once more. "But I did notice that you were looking pretty cute today."

"Oh." Andy's cheeks flamed up. He forgot all about the ball. It came bouncing down in front of him, narrowly missing his nose. "Uh, thanks."

"Yeah. Those carpenter pants look really good on you," she went on.

Andy's stomach fell. She was paying attention to how his pants fit? Suddenly he felt like he'd rather be solving calculus problems. "Thanks," he said again, trying to think of an excuse to get off the phone.

"So. When are we going out again?" she asked.

Andy picked up the ball, gripping it tightly. Man, this girl was direct. Then he remembered Evan's e-mail and felt a rush of relief. Thankfully there was a set group plan. "How about tomorrow night?" he asked. "A bunch of us are going to the Riot."

"Oh," Six said, sounding a little weird. "Yeah. Okay. Sounds fun."

"Cool," Andy responded quickly. He began to pace around his room. "Listen. I gotta go. I got to, uh, my mom's calling me." His stomach twisted as he realized how lame he sounded.

"Oh. All right. I'll see you tomorrow. Hey—good luck with your math homework."

"Yeah. You too. Bye," Andy said, then clicked off the phone and tossed it onto his bed.

He closed his eyes and let out a deep breath.

Something is definitely wrong with this situation. Andy stared at his open math notebook on the floor in front of him. *Because choosing homework over a girl is just not normal.*

"Okay, I'm going to put the lab instructions for today on the board," Mr. DeSantis, Conner's AP physics teacher, announced on Friday morning. "So just bear with me for a sec."

Conner leaned forward on his stool and rested his elbows on the high metal lab table as he stared at the back of Mr. DeSantis's head, or rather, his completely horrible comb-over. He glanced at the clock above the board. There were another forty minutes of physics left.

Conner dropped his head in his hands. He so didn't want to be here today. He so didn't want to be *anywhere.*

Last night he had barely slept, unable to stop thinking about his mom. Part of him was annoyed with her, and part of him was annoyed with himself for not being patient enough with her. He knew that Elizabeth was right—he was going to have to help his mom out in dealing with all of the changes in her life, which had to translate into some changes in his own life. But every time he thought about how his mom used to be, how negligent, how useless, he got angry all over again, and the idea of following her random rules was ridiculous.

All he knew was that being in school right now

was painful. He hoped this day would somehow go fast. Then he could go and chill out with Elizabeth and forget about everything. Conner lifted his head from his hands and looked at the clock again. Thirty-nine minutes left. No such luck.

Maria nudged him, and Conner groaned inwardly. He wasn't in the mood to chat. At least she was his lab partner and would probably take care of completing their assignment.

"Hey. How's it going?" she asked in a whisper, wrapping her long gray cardigan more tightly around her slim frame.

Conner shrugged. "Fine." He looked away to signal that he was through talking.

It went right over Maria's head. "I heard that you went over to Liz's last night," she said.

Conner glanced over at her, his eyebrows scrunching together. Was that really such a news flash?

"Oh, I spoke to her after you left," Maria explained, obviously reading the confusion in Conner's expression.

Ookay, Conner thought, nodding slightly. That still didn't explain why in the world she was bringing this up.

"All right, everyone." Mr. DeSantis turned around. He stepped away from the blackboard. "Why don't you guys take five minutes to read this over and ask me any questions you have, and then we'll get started."

"Anyway, it's good you went over," Maria whispered, leaning in closer to Conner as the rest of the class directed their attention to the blackboard.

Conner sat up straight. *It was a good thing he went over?* According to who? And what business was it of Maria's? Glancing first at Mr. DeSantis to make sure he wasn't looking their way, Conner narrowed his eyes at her. "What do you mean?"

Maria's dark eyebrows lifted as if she'd been caught at something. "Oh, nothing," she whispered, waving it off with her hand. Her eyes darted over to Mr. DeSantis, who was leaning on his desk and reading a pamphlet. "It's just that she's been kind of bummed that you haven't seen her much lately, that's all. Especially since she wants to help you out with everything that's going on at home. So it's good that you went over," she finished casually. Then she looked at the blackboard and began to read Mr. DeSantis's directions.

Conner stared at her profile in disbelief. His hands gripped onto the edge of the cold table. How did *Maria* know what was going on at home?

Is Liz walking around complaining about me or something? he wondered, gripping the table tighter. Didn't she know he had enough other crap to worry about without dealing with her nosy friends' lame input? If Elizabeth had a problem, why didn't she just come to him? Besides, Elizabeth was the one who was always too busy to see him anyway.

He felt his shoulder and neck muscles tense up.

His head pounded. *And just where does Maria get off butting in?*

"Okay, guys," Mr. DeSantis announced as everyone around the room started to chatter. "If no one has any questions, why don't you begin?"

Maria turned to Conner. She opened her spiral notebook to a clean page and pulled a pen out of her brown shoulder bag. "You ready?"

Conner's nostrils flared. *Yeah*, he thought, glaring at her. *I'm ready to get the hell out of here.*

He dropped his head into his hands once more.

This was going to be a long day.

Maria Slater

What are your career aspirations and why?

I think, at this age, it is important for me to keep my career options open. I'd like to explore many possible paths before I commit to one and limit myself.

For example, I used to think that I wanted to be a journalist. But recent experiences have showed me that I might be more suited to be a psychiatrist or therapist of some sort.

After all, you have to recognize your strengths. And I seem to have a knack for solving people's problems.

CHAPTER

Might as Well Deal with Reality

Friday after school Conner sat slumped on the brown leather couch in the small study off his living room, watching TV. He had never been much of a television fan, and he had absolutely no interest in the rerun of a dorky sitcom that was on right now. But there was nothing else he wanted to do. He just wanted to forget about everything that was going on in his life—his mom, his annoying conversation with Maria, his irritation with Elizabeth for talking to Maria in the first place—and allow his brain to turn to mush.

He rolled his eyes as the show's laugh track erupted after a particularly lame joke. *This could end up getting me even more annoyed,* he realized. Conner picked up the remote and changed the channel to MTV, where a woman in a bikini was idiotically interviewing some one-hit-wonder pop star.

"Conner?"

He glanced away from the TV to see his mom standing in the doorway, her narrow tortoiseshell reading glasses perched on the end of her nose.

Sighing, he flicked off the TV. "Hey," he said, sitting up. "What's up?"

"Not much. I was just going over our finances," she told him, walking inside. She sat down in the plaid oversized armchair next to the couch.

Conner lifted his eyebrows in surprise. That sounded promising. Before she left for rehab, Conner had been the one who'd had to deal with managing their money. Her taking over was definitely a positive sign. "Cool."

Mrs. Sandborn took off her glasses and placed them on top of her head, pushing back the stray strands of blond hair that had fallen from her bun. "Actually, I'm a little concerned."

Concern. Another good sign. "Yeah?" he asked, yawning and stretching his hands behind his head. "What about?"

"How we've been spending our money," she told him, leaning forward and clasping her hands. She gazed at Conner with a serious expression, her blue eyes unwavering. "To tell you the truth, I'm worried that you haven't been saving enough. I've noticed that a lot of our purchasing has gone toward unnecessary items."

I haven't been saving enough? Conner blinked, his muscles freezing as tension rose in every cell of his body. *She didn't just really say that, did she? Because if she did—*

"In the future, we're going to have to be a lot more careful in our spending practices," she continued.

"Don't just buy on a whim. And shop around and compare prices before we make any major purchases."

Conner stood up instantly, ready to explode. "You've got to be kidding," he snapped, glaring at her.

Mrs. Sandborn looked up at him, surprise evident in her expression. "Conner, there's no reason to get so upset," she began. "I'm just trying to—"

"No!" Conner interrupted, unable to control his rage. "If you had a problem with how I was dealing with our money, why didn't you take care of it yourself?" He threw his hands up in the air. "Oh, right. I forgot. Because you were passed out drunk half of the time."

Conner's mom's face went pale. She glanced down at the floor, and Conner could tell by the way her hands were shaking slightly that his words had stung. But he didn't care. He couldn't believe that she had the nerve to criticize how he had taken care of things while she was off drinking. She was lucky he'd been there at all.

Still, when he stared down at her now and saw her clasp and unclasp her silver-and-gold watch like she always did when she was upset and trying to hold it in, a tiny part of him felt bad. A tiny part remembered what Elizabeth had said last night.

But only a tiny part.

He stormed out of the room without another word and stalked up the stairs and into his room, slamming the door behind him. This was all so unreal. He sat on his bed, his leg bouncing up and down with pent-up energy.

Glancing at the alarm clock on his wooden dresser, he realized that he was supposed to pick up Elizabeth in about an hour. Well, that definitely wasn't going to happen. Seeing her would just remind him how annoyed he was at her for the whole Maria thing. Besides, he was far from being in the mood for a date.

Cursing under his breath, he searched around his room for the cordless phone, finally finding it under a mound of dirty clothes on the floor. He dialed Elizabeth's number.

"Hello?" Elizabeth picked up on the second ring.

At least she had been the one to answer. He couldn't deal with talking to anyone else in her family right now. "Liz. It's me."

"Conner!" she said. "Hey! When are you picking me up?"

He kicked at a stray sock on the floor. "I'm gonna have to bail on tonight, Liz. I'm not feeling too great."

"Oh, no. What's wrong?" she asked. "Do you want me to come over? I could bring some—"

"No, no," Conner broke in, not having any patience for her Florence Nightingale routine. "I just need to sleep it off and chill by myself."

"Oh," Elizabeth responded in a quiet voice. "Okay."

"I'll talk to you tomorrow, all right?" he said, really needing to get off the phone before he snapped.

There was silence for a second. Then Elizabeth said, "Yeah . . . all right."

"Okay. Bye." Conner clicked off the phone and tossed it back on the floor.

He fell back onto his bed, rubbing his eyes with the palms of his hands. He could tell that Elizabeth was hurt by the sound of her voice.

Sighing, he sat up. It wasn't his fault. She was the one who had annoyed him in the first place. Just like his mom.

Conner ran a hand through his short dark hair and groaned.

Was there a female in his life who *didn't* piss him off?

Elizabeth stared at her black cordless phone after she'd hung up with Conner. Or, more precisely, after he'd hung up *on* her. And as much as she told herself not to be, she couldn't help feeling hurt and upset at the way he'd bailed on their plans.

But he's sick, she argued with herself, walking over to her mahogany dresser and opening up the bottom drawer. *He doesn't feel well, so he wasn't in the mood to talk.* She pulled out a pair of soft cotton pajamas. If she was going to stay in tonight, she might as well get cozy.

But he was so short with me, she thought as she undressed. *And if I wasn't feeling well, I'd want nothing more than to have him come over and hang out.*

She sighed, grabbing a black scrunchie off the top of her dresser and gathering her shoulder-length hair into a ponytail. *But he's not you,* she thought. She stared at her dismal reflection in the oval mirror above her dresser. *We're totally different people.*

Unfortunately Elizabeth already knew that all too well.

Elizabeth also couldn't stop a nagging thought from invading her brain. *Did he call Tia?* she wondered. And if he did, was he having a longer conversation with her than he'd had with Elizabeth?

"Hey, Liz, what's with the pj's?" Jessica asked, walking into the room. At the moment the identical sisters couldn't look more different. Jessica was decked out in black hip huggers, a gray halter top, and a radiant smile. "Aren't you going out with Conner tonight?"

"He canceled," she said quietly. "He's sick."

"Bummer," Jessica responded. Stepping next to Elizabeth, she grabbed the Delish lip gloss off the dresser. "So come out with me, then," Jessica suggested as she applied the almost clear lipstick. "A bunch of us are going to the Riot, remember?" She smacked her lips together. "It'll be fun."

Elizabeth walked over to her sleigh bed and plopped down on it. She had been looking forward to a romantic night alone with Conner. The idea of hanging out in a crowded, noisy club when she was now in such a cranky mood was beyond unappealing. "I don't think I feel like it, Jess. Thanks, though."

Jessica turned to look at Elizabeth, frowning. "You all right?" she asked. "Are you mad at Conner or something?"

"No, no," Elizabeth said, bringing her legs up onto the bed Indian style. She knew she was wrong for being annoyed with him to begin with—after all, the guy *was* sick—and the last thing she wanted to do was overanalyze the situation with her twin. "I'm just tired, that's all."

"All right." Jessica shrugged, turning back to the mirror. She ran a hand through her straight hair, rearranging it. "But I'm not leaving for twenty minutes. So you can think about it."

"Okay." Elizabeth bit her lip as she watched her sister. Suddenly, out of nowhere, it was really important for her to know if Tia was going to the Riot too. Because if she wasn't, that could mean that she and Conner were . . . *No, stop it,* Elizabeth thought. *Stop being so stupidly jealous. Conner's sick. Period.*

"If you change your mind, let me know," Jessica said, heading for Elizabeth's door.

"Hey, Jess," Elizabeth blurted out, fidgeting with her necklace. "Is, uh, is Tia going to be there tonight?"

"I think Evan mentioned she's planning on coming." Jessica crossed her tanned arms over her chest. "Why?"

"No reason. Just wondering," Elizabeth responded, trying to sound as casual as possible.

Jessica squinted at Elizabeth. "Liz? Are you sure you're all right? Does this have something to do with Tia and Conner?"

Elizabeth rolled her eyes. "Nooo," she said, drawing the word out to emphasize it.

Jessica nodded, watching Elizabeth carefully. "Whatever you say. But if you need me, you know where I am. Okay?"

Elizabeth sighed dramatically, as if to show Jessica that she was being ridiculous. Which, of course, she wasn't. But she didn't need to know that. "Okay."

"Good." Jessica nodded again, then headed out the door.

Elizabeth fell back on her bed, lying flat on her back.

So Tia was going to be at the Riot. At least that meant that Conner wasn't going to be with her. He really did want to be alone.

Elizabeth brought her legs up to her chest, curling up into a ball.

Somehow, though, that didn't exactly make her feel any better.

"Okay, okay, I got one," Andy announced a couple of hours later at the Riot. He was sitting at a large, round table that he'd secured in one corner of the loud, packed club with Six, Maria, Ken, Evan, and Jessica. For the past fifteen minutes they had been entrenched in a game of "Would you rather?"

Andy leaned forward, scanning his friends' faces. "Would you rather go out with someone who is the most beautiful person on earth but is also the dumbest one or someone who is very smart but uglier than you can imagine?"

"Oh God," Maria interjected, rolling her eyes. "This is the most idiotic game. It's not like you'd ever have to make that kind of decision in real life."

Andy laughed. Maria had said practically the same thing after every question that someone asked. She was sort of missing the point. "But say that you did," he persisted, wrapping his hands around his cold glass of Coke. "Who would you choose?"

"That's easy." Maria shifted her position on Ken's lap, pulling down on her knee-length brown skirt. "The guy who's smart but ugly."

"Really?" Ken asked, looking up at her.

"Of course," Maria responded. "I could never go out with someone who's dumb."

Ken grinned. "I'll take that as a compliment."

"I agree with Maria," Evan piped in. He sat back in his chair, letting one skinny arm drape down the back of it. "That's a no-brainer, Andy."

"I don't think you guys realize that we're talking about the *ugliest person in the world* here. Repulsive. Scary looking," Andy argued. He didn't understand how they could say that they would go out with someone that they didn't find attractive. *After all, I'm going out with someone that I do find attractive, and I'm still not attracted to her,* he thought, looking at everyone except Six, who was sitting right next to him.

"Yeah," Jessica agreed, nudging Evan. "How can you kiss someone who repulses you?"

"How can *you* kiss someone who can't carry on a conversation?" Evan retorted. He took a sip of his soda, then shook his head. "You know what? Don't answer that."

Six giggled. "Evan, come on. Brains are important,

139

but you have to admit that pure physical attraction is too. You can't really have a relationship without it."

Suddenly Andy's face felt very hot. He was *not* comfortable with the turn the conversation had taken. *Idiot,* he thought. *Why did you ask that stupid question in the first place?*

"Hey, everyone," a guy's voice called out.

Andy glanced up. It was Travis, in his usual worn-out flannel and khaki shorts, with two guys who looked vaguely familiar from school. Andy was more than happy to see him. *Just in time,* he thought, thankful for the distraction.

Everyone at the table said their hellos, and Travis introduced his two friends, Mike and Kwame, and explained that they were going backpacking with him this summer.

"So, you guys just hanging out?" Travis asked after his friends walked over to the bar to buy some drinks.

"Actually, we were playing a really stupid game," Maria explained, sliding off Ken's lap. "Here. Take our seat," she told Travis, pulling Ken up with her arm. "I've had enough. I gotta dance."

She walked off. Ken shrugged to his friends, then followed her. Travis dropped into the chair they had been sitting in—the one on the other side of Andy. "What was that about?" Travis asked.

"Uh, never mind. Not important." Andy popped an ice cube in his mouth and crunched down on it, trying to think of something witty to say to change the topic of conversation. "So. Are your plans all settled for your trip?" *Nice one, Marsden,* he thought, mentally kicking himself. *He's going to think that's all you can talk about. Like you're some kind of Europe groupie or something.*

"As much as they're gonna be." Travis tilted his chair on its back two legs, keeping his balance by holding on to the edge of the table. "We have our airline tickets and Eurail passes. The rest we're gonna make up as we go along."

"Wow." Andy stared back at him, once again superjealous of the voyage he was about to take. And truthfully, he was also superjealous of Travis. The guy just seemed so with it. So together, but in a completely laid-back way. "That's very cool."

Six pushed Andy back from his leaning-forward position so that she could see her brother. "I thought you were going to the movies tonight," she said.

Travis shrugged. "We were. It was sold out."

"So how long do you think you're going to be gone for?" Andy asked, changing the subject back to the one that interested him. For some reason, he loved the way Travis talked about his plans.

"I'm not sure," Travis responded, dropping the chair back to its normal position. "Maybe six weeks."

Andy was just opening his mouth to ask Travis something else when Six tapped him. "Andy! It's like you want to talk to my brother more than you want to talk to me."

Andy reddened at the observation. It was true. What was he supposed to say to that?

141

"Come on," Six went on, standing up and tugging on Andy's arm. "Let's dance." She glanced at her brother. "I'm getting just a little sick of hearing about your trip. No offense," she teased.

Travis held up his hands in surrender. "Hey. None taken." He looked at Andy and nodded. "Go ahead. Boogie on."

Andy looked from Travis to Six and realized that he didn't have a choice. Six was bouncing up and down as she pulled on his arm, her green eyes determined.

"All right," Andy said, standing up. Six smiled, then turned around, heading for the throng of dancing people in the center of the room. Andy followed, admiring how she looked from behind in her tight white capri pants and blue scoop-neck top.

I've got to get it together, he thought, watching her. *She is beautiful. I can't screw this up more than I already have.*

She picked a spot on the dance floor, and Andy danced up next to her, resolving to show her that they could have a fun time together. But after a moment of dancing, Six stepped closer to Andy. And closer.

Too close. She was practically rubbing up against him, in a very sexy, MTV-ish way. There was just one problem. It was not turning Andy on. Not at all. In fact, it was having the opposite effect.

He took a step back, but Six simply moved up close to him again.

Andy tried to ignore how uncomfortable he was as he danced with Six for a couple more moments.

But his uneasiness was causing his movements to be stiff and awkward, and after a minute he couldn't fake it any longer.

You can't lead her on like this any longer, Marsden, Andy told himself. *It's not fair.* Of course, the right thing to do would have been to let her know how he felt right then and there, but Andy knew that there was no way he could handle that. Not with all his friends sitting back at the table to watch the melt-down. So he did the next-best thing.

"Hey, Six?" he said, freezing in place and tugging on the collar of his long-sleeve Quiksilver T-shirt. "I'm sorry, but I'm kinda tired. Can we sit back down?"

Six stopped moving as well. Total disappointment. "Already?"

I can't break up with her, Andy thought, taking in her upset expression. How could he hurt her like that?

"Yeah. Sorry. I just, uh, had a long day," he lied, stuffing his hands in his pockets.

Six sighed, dropping her hands at her sides. "Okay. Sure."

"Cool," Andy responded, leading her off the dance floor. As they headed back to the table, he eyed the empty seat next to Travis.

At least he knew that he'd have a good time chilling out with Travis. And at the moment that was exactly what Andy needed.

Elizabeth Wakefield

<u>Reasons</u> <u>that</u> <u>I</u> shouldn't <u>be</u> <u>worried</u>
<u>about</u> <u>Conner</u> <u>and</u> <u>Tia</u>

They've always spent a lot of time together—this is nothing new

Tia and Angel just broke up—Tia isn't ready to jump into another relationship

They're best friends—they don't think of each other that way

Tia would never do that to me

Conner would never cheat on me

<u>Reasons</u> <u>that</u> <u>I</u> should <u>be</u> <u>worried</u>
<u>about</u> <u>Conner</u> <u>and</u> <u>Tia</u>

They've been spending <u>a</u> <u>lot</u> of time together

Tia and Angel just broke up—Tia might be lonely

They're best friends—the perfect basis for a relationship

Tia _might_ do that to me—after all, I did it to Maria, right?

How do I know that Conner would never cheat on me?

Tia wrapped her cozy white terry-cloth robe around her body after stepping out of the shower. She towel dried her long, wavy hair for a moment, then walked out of her bathroom and into her bedroom.

And almost smacked right into Conner.

"God! Conner!" she exclaimed, her heart leaping to her throat and beating about one million pulses per second. She took a deep breath to calm herself down, holding her hand to her chest. "You really have to stop doing that!"

"Sorry," Conner said. He leaned against the edge of her dresser and stuffed his left hand into the front pocket of his Levi's. "Your window was open."

"Well, that doesn't mean you can just bust right in," she ranted, putting her hands on her hips.

"Okay, okay, I'm sorry, Tee." Conner looked down at the carpet, then back up at her. "I had to get out of my house."

Tia's anger disappeared at the sound of Conner's voice—it sounded so flat. Dejected. Like he really needed to talk. His green eyes looked flat too. Tired.

He was wearing a dark blue T-shirt that she'd never seen him in before. Somehow the color perfectly accented his complexion and eyes, making him look really . . . *hot*. She saw his eyes fall on the exposed part of her naked chest and shoulder, where her bathrobe had slipped off a little.

She immediately crashed back to reality. *This is Conner*. Conner, she reminded herself. *Your friend—just like Liz is your friend*. She felt her cheeks flush, and she closed her bathrobe tighter, pulling on its belt. "I thought you were going out with Liz."

"I couldn't deal with her tonight," he said, walking over to Tia's desk. He picked up a silver-framed black-and-white photo of Tia and her brother Miguel as little kids and stared at it. "I told her I was sick."

Tia's mouth fell open. This was exactly what Maria had been warning her about. Elizabeth was going to hate her before long. "No, no, no, you can't stay here." She hurried over to him, lifting the frame from his hands and leading him over to the window. "Liz would lose it if she found that you ditched her and hung out with me instead."

Conner froze, resisting Tia's tugs to get him out. "Screw Liz!" he exclaimed. "This isn't about her." Surprised by his harsh tone, Tia let go of his arm. "God," he went on through clenched teeth, his face getting red. "What is this? Now I can't even talk to my best friend?"

Whoa. Something must be up, Tia thought as she

148

blinked back at him. He was showing some serious hostility. "Hey, Conner, I'm sorry," she told him softly, squeezing his arm. "Calm down, all right?"

Conner sighed. "Yeah." He walked over to Tia's bed and sat down on the edge of it, resting his elbows on his knees and hanging his head. "I'm just totally exhausted from everything that's gone on lately." He looked up at Tia. "All I want to do is veg out and watch mindless TV. Okay?"

Tia bit her lip as she stared back at him. She *was* supposed to go to the Riot tonight to meet up with everyone else, but Conner looked so miserable. More miserable than she'd seen him in a while, if that was even possible.

And anyway, she thought, fidgeting with her bathrobe's belt, *I'm more in the mood to just chill out with him than have a late night out with everyone else.*

Of course, there was still the small problem that Tia had been feeling the teensiest bit attracted to Conner lately. *But nothing would ever happen,* she reasoned, walking over to sit down next to him. *Because that would be insane.*

"Yeah, okay," she told him, pushing her hair behind her shoulders. "I could deal with a mellow night myself."

"Cool," Conner said. He turned to her and gave her shoulder a quick massage with one hand. "Thanks."

"No problem," Tia responded, nodding.

Yup. Everything was going to be just fine. That is,

if she could just ignore the tingles that shot up from her spine at Conner's touch. . . .

"Door-to-door service," Andy announced as he pulled into Six's wide gravel driveway, right next to her front door. Six had been uncharacteristically quiet tonight after they'd stopped dancing, and Andy knew it was all his fault. It probably hadn't helped much that he had spent most of the night talking to Travis either. So now he was trying to lighten the mood, attempting to joke around, but failing miserably and sounding forced and goofy instead.

But Six smiled—a genuine smile—her eyes lighting up, and Andy grinned back at her, relaxing somewhat. Before he could say anything more, Six met his gaze and leaned forward, obviously to kiss him.

Andy immediately went into panic mode. He didn't know what his problem was, but he just didn't want to kiss her. Period. So Andy kept his mouth tightly shut, and when their lips met, he only gave Six a quick peck before moving away.

Freak, he thought, cursing himself for pulling yet another wimp move. *What's your deal?* His ears burning up, Andy gripped the edge of his faux-leather car seat and looked down.

"Well, good night," he said, trying to adopt a casual tone. He knew he'd just disappointed her again, but hopefully she wouldn't voice it. He didn't think he could deal with it right now. He was way too confused.

So Andy knew that she liked him more than he liked her, but what was the big deal? Why couldn't he handle just a small kiss?

"Andy? Could you please tell me what's wrong?" Six asked, a clearly annoyed edge to her voice.

Wish I knew, he thought, squeezing the car seat tighter.

Six sighed and looked away. She played with the lock on the car door. "You really *aren't* attracted to me, are you?" she said quietly.

Andy's stomach muscles tightened. How could he have this discussion when he didn't even know how he really felt? He brought his hands up to the steering wheel and faced forward. "No, that's not it. I told you already. I'm just tired," he said as another car pulled up next to them.

"I know, but . . . ," Six began, letting her voice trail off. She stared down at her lap.

Andy turned all the way around to face her, suddenly feeling horrible as he saw the way she was biting her bottom lip and fidgeting like crazy, clearly trying to control her emotions. *Say something to her,* he thought. *Lie, okay? Just lie.*

But just as he was about to open his mouth to tell her something comforting, he noticed that Travis was getting out of the black Ford Explorer that was now parked next to them.

Andy watched, inexplicably intrigued, as Travis locked his car door, flipping his longish blond hair back off his face.

Andy took in everything, from Travis's loose flannel shirt to his Birkenstock sandals. And then the oddest thing happened. Andy's heart skipped a beat. It actually *skipped* a beat.

What the hell? Andy's palms began to sweat. Looking away from Travis, he gripped the steering wheel tighter, his pulse racing like crazy. He suddenly felt sick to his stomach.

What was going on?

Travis turned around and saw Andy and Six. He lifted his chin, giving them a small smile. "Hey, good night, guys," he called before jogging into the house.

Andy stared after him, still feeling nauseous. He was completely unable to wrap his brain around what had just happened. Or hadn't happened.

Maybe that didn't *really happen,* Andy thought. *Maybe I'm going crazy.*

"Andy, are you all right?" Six asked. "You look . . . ill."

Andy turned to face her, his hands still holding on to the steering wheel for dear life. "Yeah, uh, actually, I don't feel so hot," he told her. "I think I gotta go."

Six's eyes opened wide as she searched his face. "Wow, you really are sick," she told him, placing a hand on his forehead. "You're all clammy. No wonder you're so tired."

"Yeah," was all Andy could reply. His brain was too crowded with thoughts of Travis and then rapid denials of those thoughts. He definitely was losing his mind. *Get a grip, Marsden.*

"Well, feel better, okay?" Six said. She gave him a

quick kiss on his cheek. "Get lots of sleep. Good night."

Andy was silent. He barely noticed as Six opened the car door and stepped outside, hurrying into her house.

In fact, he barely noticed *anything* as he sat there, frozen in his car for the next few minutes, going over and over in his mind what had just happened.

And then praying that it hadn't.

Conner opened his eyes and was instantly confused. *Where am I?* he wondered, staring up at the familiar ceiling with a pale pink border around the moldings. Then he noticed the television flashing in front of the four-poster bed that he was lying on, and he remembered.

He was at Tia's. They must have fallen asleep watching TV. The clock on the VCR said it was three forty-two.

Should I go home? he wondered, feeling disoriented and groggy.

Propping up his head, he saw that Tia was sound asleep next to him, lying on her side and curled up into a ball, her little feet just barely touching his legs.

Conner smiled to himself at the sight. She looked so . . . peaceful, her body rising and falling slightly as she breathed. Her face was always so full of energy that it was kind of cool to see her at rest.

He watched her silently for a moment, taking in her insanely long, dark eyelashes as he debated whether or not to leave.

Nah, he decided finally, realizing that if he got up, he'd probably wake her too. And after she had been so there for him tonight, helping him completely forget about everything, she deserved to sleep undisturbed.

Besides, he was pretty comfortable anyway.

And without a second thought, he dropped his head back and closed his eyes.

TIA RAMIREZ

OKAY. FINE. I ADMIT IT. I'VE BEEN KIND OF ATTRACTED TO CONNER LATELY. THERE. I SAID IT. ALL RIGHT?

BUT I MEAN, IT'S REALLY NOT A BIG DEAL. IT'S DEFINITELY NOT ANYTHING TO WORRY ABOUT.

FIRST OF ALL, I'M SURE THE ONLY REASON THAT I'VE AT ALL BEEN THINKING ABOUT CONNER IN A SEXUAL WAY IS BECAUSE I MISS ANGEL. I'M LONELY WITHOUT HIM. SO FOR NOW, CONNER IS FILLING THAT SPACE IN MY BRAIN. BUT IT'S ALL JUST IN MY HEAD. IT'S NOT LIKE I'M GOING TO JUMP HIM OR ANYTHING.

ALSO, IT'S COMPLETELY NORMAL. FACE IT. CONNER'S A GOOD-LOOKING GUY. I'M A GIRL. AND I'M NOT BLIND. PERIOD. THAT'S ALL THERE IS TO IT.

AND IT'S NOT LIKE I'M <u>CONSTANTLY</u> ATTRACTED TO HIM.

THERE ARE JUST CERTAIN FLEETING
MOMENTS WHEN I LOOK AT HIM IN
THAT WAY, AND THEN THEY
DISAPPEAR. BUT AS LONG AS I
HAVE THOSE MOMENTS UNDER
CONTROL—AND I DO—THERE'S NO
CAUSE FOR CONCERN.

REALLY.

Andy Marsden

A list of possible reasons as to why my heart starting to beat irregularly fast when I saw Travis tonight:

I have a heart condition (note to self: Check that out)

I drank too much coffee today (highly possible, by the way)

Six had me so worked up from all her questions—the heart beating was just an aftereffect

I've been working too hard (doubtful, but still possible, all right?)

I need to get more, or even some, exercise

CHAPTER 11
A New Woman

Andy prayed that his mom wouldn't be waiting up for him as he unlocked his front door that night. She always did wait up, but maybe tonight, by some miracle, she was too tired to stay awake. He knew he couldn't deal with talking to her, given everything that he was going through.

"Hi, sweetie! How was your night?" Mrs. Marsden called out from her seat on the couch in the living room the minute Andy's foot stepped into the foyer.

Andy closed the door behind him. Luck wasn't exactly streaming his way these days, was it?

"Fine," he said, heading straight for the stairs.

His mom put her book down on the coffee table and walked over to him, taking off her reading glasses and setting them on top of her head. "And how are things going with Six?" she pressed, the corners of her mouth curving into a slight smile.

Andy rolled his eyes. As if the problem he was now grappling with was something he could discuss with his mother. *Great, Mom. Except for the tiny problem that I'm more attracted to her brother than I am to her.* "Fine," he responded, making no effort to disguise his annoyance.

Mrs. Marsden held up her hands in surrender. "I know, I know," she said with a laugh. "This is not something you want to talk about with me."

Bingo, Andy thought, inching his way up the stairs.

His mother grinned, sizing him up with her small brown eyes. "I just think it's wonderful that you finally have a girlfriend."

"Uh-huh," Andy responded, his stomach twisting in about a million different directions. He turned around and headed up the stairs. He couldn't stand this for a minute longer. There was no accounting for what he might say. "Night," he called from the upstairs hallway.

"Good night, dear," his mom called back, her voice still sounding unusually chipper.

Wonderful. She's already planning the wedding. Andy bolted into his room and shut the door behind him. Could he just stay in here forever?

Andy took off his corduroy jacket and threw it on the floor—where most of his clothes lay in overflowing piles—and then sank down into his desk chair, dropping his head into his hands.

Andy knew he shouldn't even bother to get into bed that night. If he did, he'd end up just lying there, staring up at the ceiling with his eyes wide open and his body stiff, like he always did when he had a lot on his mind.

And man, did he have a lot on his mind tonight.

Too much to even touch his Nintendo. Andy trudged over to his window and stared out at the tall palm trees rustling in the wind in front of his house.

The thing was, Andy had always known that he wasn't interested in girls in the same way that his friends were. But he'd just figured that simply meant that his hormones were more in check than the average teenage guy's. And that he hadn't met the right girl yet. But when he finally did find her, he'd be like everyone else.

Andy's stomach twisted and turned again as Tia's words from the other day replayed themselves in his brain. *When you're attracted to someone, you'll know.*

His knees feeling shaky, Andy turned and sat down on top of his desk. The truth was, if he was one hundred percent honest with himself, he knew he'd had the same kind of weird feeling that he'd had with Travis tonight with other guys in the past. But he'd always pushed those brief thoughts away as fast as possible—he'd never let himself dwell on them. And he'd certainly never let him consider the idea that he might be . . . Andy swallowed, wringing his hands.

That he might be gay.

Andy let out a deep breath, wiping his sweaty palms on his jeans. He wasn't even sure now. He wasn't sure of *anything.* His entire view of the world was turned upside down.

Andy stood up again. He began to pace around

161

his room. At the moment there was only one thing that he did know for sure. He had to break things off with Six.

After all, she deserved a guy who really wanted her and would make her feel special.

Andy kicked a mound of dirty clothes. He closed his eyes.

And he was definitely not that guy.

Ken woke up relatively early the next morning, especially considering that he hadn't gotten home until late the night before.

I must just be pumped up for today, he thought, throwing off his thick green comforter. He and Maria were driving out to Malibu, where Maria's aunt had a phat house on a bluff overlooking the beach—the kind of house that graced the pages of an architectural magazine. He and Maria had planned to get an early start to make the most of their day of luxury, and Ken was raring to go.

As he stepped out of bed and onto the carpet, he heard a woman humming in the bathroom next to his room. Ken smiled. *Asha.* By the sounds of her, she was in as good a mood as he was. And Ken was glad. He grinned as he realized that he was actually happy to have her around.

Ken quickly pulled on a white T-shirt and a pair of khaki shorts, then headed downstairs to grab a glass of orange juice before calling Maria.

His father was already in the kitchen, sitting in

the breakfast nook and reading the *Sweet Valley Tribune* with his back to Ken. And he was also . . . *humming?*

Ken blinked. He had never heard his father hum in his life.

Then Ken noticed his father's framed award sitting on the countertop. He smiled. *Guess the gift went over well,* he thought, mentally patting himself on the back for helping Asha out with everything.

"Have a good date last night?" Ken asked lightly as he crossed the kitchen to take the orange juice out of the refrigerator.

Mr. Matthews glanced up from the paper, startled. "Oh, hi, Ken." He put down the paper and took a sip of his coffee. "Actually, yes. We had fun."

Ken arched an eyebrow as he reached for a glass from the overhead cabinet. "Really?"

"Mmm. Tried this new Moroccan place on North Pico. Very festive."

Whoa. That was more information than Ken's father had divulged in years. Ken poured some juice into his glass. "How so?" he asked.

"Well, let's see. There was plenty of loud music," Mr. Matthews began. He let out a short chuckle. "And a couple of belly dancers."

Ken watched his father in amazement as he continued to drink his coffee. Humming, belly dancers? He was like a changed man.

Ken shook his head as he heard Asha's footsteps coming down the stairs. He definitely needed to congratulate the woman on a job well done. *I mean, it hasn't been that long, and Dad's already chilling out,* he thought. *So what if—*

Ken's thoughts were abruptly cut off, and he almost dropped his glass on the tiled floor.

Because at the moment his father's date from last night was strolling into the kitchen and planting a kiss on the top of Mr. Matthews's head.

But she was blond, short, and blue-eyed.

And definitely not Asha.

It was a bright, clear, sunny Saturday morning, and Elizabeth felt like a new woman as she drove over to Conner's house in the Jeep. She turned the radio up loud, bopping her head to the music. Then, braking at a red light, she smiled at a group of cute little kids who were crossing the street in front of her on their bikes. Yep. It was going to be a great day. Thankfully, after getting to bed early last night and having a solid night of sleep, Elizabeth had woken up refreshed. Relaxed. And happier.

I was so pathetic last night, she thought, pressing on the gas and wincing as she remembered how she had played the part of the clingy girlfriend.

After all, she reasoned as she drove past the Corner Market and the video store that weren't far from Conner's house, *I like the fact that Conner and I have the kind of relationship where we're independent and don't* always *have to be together.* And it was a total Conner move to want to be alone when he was sick. She shouldn't have been so upset and dramatic about it.

She shrugged and grinned to herself as she made a left turn down Conner's street. Well, that was all over and done with. Now she was going to surprise Conner with a rare morning visit, armed with some onion bagels and freshly squeezed orange juice from Ben's Bagels—the best bagel store in Sweet Valley. Hopefully Conner would be feeling better. If not, well, Elizabeth would just have to make him.

She pulled into Conner's driveway and parked. Grabbing her white paper bag, she stepped out of her car and jogged up to Conner's front door.

I wonder if his mom'll be here, she thought as she rang the doorbell. She hadn't considered the possibility until now, and the idea made her a little nervous. She wasn't quite sure how she should act around her.

Luckily Megan answered the door.

"Liz! Hi," Megan said, her half-closed, sleepy-looking eyes opening wider. She pushed tangled strawberry-blond hair away from her face. "What are you doing here so early?" Then she eyed the paper bag that Elizabeth was holding. She peered into it. "Hey. Did you bring me breakfast?"

Elizabeth lifted up her sunglasses, placing them on top of her head and pushing back her blond hair. "Yes. Well, you *and* Conner." She grinned.

Megan shook her head as she leaned against the frame of the doorway. "I just went into his room.

165

He's not here," she said, yawning. "Actually, come to think of it, I'm not sure if he even ever came home last night."

What? Elizabeth's heart took a tumble dive onto the concrete step. "Came home?" she repeated, feeling queasy. "I thought he was sick."

Megan stood up straight. "Uh, no," she said, fidgeting with the hem of her white V-necked T-shirt. She bit her lip. "I mean, I don't think he was," she continued. "He went out, but I'm not sure where."

Elizabeth felt like a knife had been plunged into her gut. He had gone *out?* After he'd told her he was sick? *He lied to me,* she thought, clenching on to the paper bag with all of her strength. And then another even more horrible thought entered her brain. One that made her feel like she actually might faint.

Is he at Tia's?

"Liz?" Megan said, squeezing her arm. "Please don't get all upset. I might be wrong. I mean, Conner might've been sick and then went out anyway. Or maybe he—"

"I have to go," Elizabeth cut in, feeling like her knees might buckle at any moment.

She turned around and ran back to her car, not listening as Megan called after her.

She could barely hear her anyway because only one sound filled her ears.

The superfast beating of her own heart.

Six Hanson

I've never had a problem with self-confidence. And I could never relate to those dorky articles in teen magazines that tell you how to raise your self-esteem. And I've never, ever understood those girls who are always complaining about their body, or their nose, or who think that they'll never have a boyfriend.

I like myself. I know I'm cool and fun to be around. I've never worried about whether I would meet a guy or not.

So, now that I actually _have_ met someone, I should be more confident than ever, right?

Huh. Maybe it's time to pick up one of those articles. . . .

"I don't really know how to say this," Andy began, staring down at his hands. It was Saturday morning, and he was sitting on a metal bench next to Six in the middle of Sawyer Lane Park, a small, square expanse of green a couple of blocks away from Six's house. Andy had figured that this would be the best place to meet Six to do the deed. First of all, there was no way he could handle the risk of bumping into Travis if he went over to her place to talk to her. Also, the park was safe, neutral territory. The perfect breakup venue.

"You don't want to go out with me anymore," Six finished for him.

Andy glanced up at her, his mouth falling slightly open. And when he took in her slumping shoulders and saw the way she was nervously chewing on the inside of her lip, his first instinct was to lie. Deny everything. But he knew he couldn't. Not any longer. "How did you know?"

Six rolled her eyes and let out a short, tight laugh, hugging herself. "After the way you acted last night, I didn't exactly think you asked me here to have a surprise picnic."

Andy swallowed. "Look, Six, I'm really sorry about that. I don't know what's wrong with me," he went on, his earlobes burning as he recalled all of the confusing thoughts that had been darting through his head since last night. "I'm just . . . I, uh, I just don't—"

"You just don't like me. I know," Six cut in, vigorously nodding, her strawberry-blond ponytail bopping up and down. She picked a twig up off the ground and played with it, staring down at the little stick as if it were the most interesting thing she'd ever seen. "That's cool. I understand."

You so don't *understand,* Andy thought. I *don't even understand.*

"I do like you," he insisted. "I think you're awesome. And beautiful." Six finally looked up from the twig, her green eyes softening a bit. Andy sighed. This was so hard. "Just, I guess, not . . . not in that way."

Six nodded again. Her focus went back to the twig. She bent it, then broke the stick in half. "Yeah. I figured as much."

Andy stared at the broken twig, thankful that Six had an object other than him to take her emotions out on. "I'm sorry," he said again, at a total loss for words.

Six tossed the twig onto the freshly cut grass lawn in front of them. She looked at Andy and shrugged, a trace of a sad smile on her lips. "It's okay, Andy. Really. I can handle it."

Andy felt a rush of relief. She looked like she really meant it. "Good. Cool," he said, leaning back on the bench. Feeling full of nervous energy, he rubbed his hands up and down against his legs. "And, uh, listen, not to sound like a cliché or anything, but I still want to hang out. You know, be friends." He winced inwardly as he heard himself.

Six nodded. "Yeah, definitely," she said, sounding a little *too* cheery. "Me too."

There was an uncomfortable, heavy silence for a moment as they both just looked at each other. Andy glanced away, staring down at his lap. *What am I supposed to do?* he wondered. *Is there some sort of postbreakup protocol?* He hoped not because all he wanted to do now was go home and be alone for a while.

"Well, I guess I should get going," Six said finally. Adjusting the straps of her overalls, she stood. "So . . . I'll see you on Monday, right?"

"Yeah," Andy told her, forcing a grin. "Monday."

Six nodded once more, then turned around, walking toward the curb.

Andy sat there frozen as he watched her leave, a lump forming in his throat. And for the second time in two days, he felt sick to his stomach.

He knew it was partly because he had just hurt Six, and that made him feel horrible.

But he knew it was also because there was something he now had to face.

And he sure as hell didn't want to.

Conner opened his eyes at the sound of a lawn mower outside. He was met with a burst of glaring sunshine, and he scrunched his eyes shut again.

Apparently he and Tia had not only slept with the window open last night, but they had also fallen asleep with the window *shade* open, thereby allowing all of this bright, invasive sunlight in way too early.

Not that Conner knew what time it was. It just *felt* way too early, given his exhausted and sleepy state. He was about to turn over onto his other side, away from the window, when he felt the weight draped over him. The weight of someone else's body.

Opening his eyes just the minimum amount so that he could see, he glanced down and saw a thin arm flung across his waist. Tia was using him as a human pillow. This wasn't going to work. Conner needed to turn his back on the offensive sunshine. Now.

Lifting up Tia's arm, Conner turned onto his other side so that he was facing her. He let go of her arm, expecting her to take it back or wake up, but instead, as if she were a doll, her arm simply dropped down on top of him again.

Conner opened his eyes wider. Tia was sound asleep, and she *looked* like a delicate doll, her thick, dark hair splayed all around her.

"Hey, Tee," he whispered so he could tell her to rearrange her sleeping position.

No response.

Conner smiled slightly. He'd forgotten that the girl could sleep through anything. Like the time that they went camping when they were twelve, and everyone in the tent was freaking out over what sounded like a wolf outside. Tia snored through the whole thing.

"Hey, sleeping beauty," he whispered, a little more loudly this time. He nudged her shoulder.

Her eyes slowly fluttered open. When she saw Conner, her smooth, wide forehead crinkled and her mouth formed into a pout. "I'm sleeping," she mumbled, closing her eyes again.

Not to mention that she was also a grump in the morning. "Uh-huh. On me," Conner told her.

Tia opened her eyes again. A sleepy smile crept across her face. "So?" she said. "You got a problem with that?"

Conner smiled back at her. Unbelievable. The girl had attitude first thing in the morning. She also had something else, he realized as he squinted through his half-closed eyes at her. *Like a really sexy look,* he thought as he took in the way the rays of sun were highlighting strands of her hair and the light brown flecks in her eyes.

Man, he thought, blinking. *Where did* that *come from?* This was *Tia.* He couldn't be having that kind of thought about her.

173

He opened his eyes even more and stared at her for a moment longer, though, unable to break his gaze. Why was he suddenly *so* attracted to her? Why did he want to—

Tia's eyebrows scrunched together. "Conner?"

And then, before Conner even knew what he was doing, he leaned forward. And touched his lips to hers.

Tia didn't respond. She didn't move. She just lay there.

Oh, man, Conner thought as he kissed her, his heart thumping against his rib cage. *What am I doing? I can't be doing this.*

He quickly pulled away, his breath coming out in short gasps. "Sorry," he mumbled, not knowing what had possessed him.

But Tia didn't protest. She shook her head slightly and opened her brown eyes wider, silently inviting him to kiss her again.

And even though a tiny voice in his brain was screaming at him to stop, Tia's was an invitation he couldn't refuse. Not when he was feeling the way he was. And not when Tia was *looking* the way she was.

So Conner ignored his brain, and he kissed her again.

Wow, was all Tia could think as she kissed Conner. Her heart pounded in her ears, her skin tingled with excitement, and her mind floated up to the ceiling as she lost herself in this insane, electrifying kiss.

It just felt so . . . perfect. So right, even though there were a million reasons why this was very wrong.

But for some reason *because* this was Conner, it made the kiss that much more incredible. Conner knew her better than anyone, and it somehow seemed that he even knew how she liked to be kissed.

So Tia forgot everything as she went on kissing Conner.

She forgot that Conner was her best friend. Forgot that he had a girlfriend. Forgot that his girlfriend was Elizabeth.

All she remembered as her lips melded to his was how good it felt to kiss him. She felt like she was suspended in space as her pulse continued to race at warp speed.

Somewhere in the background she vaguely heard the muted sounds of morning occurring around her. The lawn mower outside. The clanging of dishes in the kitchen. Her mother's laughter. Miguel's voice, followed by the sound of him answering the front door. A knocking on the door.

Tia's shoulders stiffened up. Her body froze. Wait. Was that knock on *her* door?

She quickly pulled away from Conner.

But she was too late. Her door had already been swung open.

175

And *Elizabeth* was standing in the doorway. She was paler than a cotton ball, and she looked like she'd just been slapped.

Tia's stomach dropped to the floor. She opened her mouth to say something, but her mouth was dry. No words came out. Besides, what *would* she say?

"Liz," Tia heard Conner croak out.

Elizabeth shook her head. Her bottom lip began to tremble. Then the tears began to stream down her cheeks.

And then she turned and ran.

Tia swallowed, clutching onto her sheets and staring at the empty doorway, trying to understand how this horribly surreal moment could have just happened. *No. It's a nightmare,* she thought, feeling strangely numb. *It has to be.*

And then the nightmare got worse.

"Tee?" Tia's mom called.

Before Tia could tell Conner to hide, before she could do *anything,* Tia's mom came into her room. And the minute she saw Conner on the bed next to Tia, she freaked.

"Tia Ramirez! What in God's name is going on?" she yelled, her face hardening and her big eyes narrowing into angry slits. "You have some explaining to do, young lady!"

At that moment Tia just wanted to die. Because for her right now, it was a better option than being alive.

ELIZABETH WAKEFIELD

9:31 A.M.

Please. Tell me I didn't just see that.
I did <u>not</u> see that. Tell me this is a
nightmare. Please!

TIA RAMIREZ

9:31 A.M.

OH GOD. WHAT THE HELL
HAPPENED? TELL ME I DIDN'T
JUST DO THAT, THAT U2 DIDN'T
JUST SEE THAT. OH. GOD.

CONNER MCDERMOTT
9:31 A.M.

Toast. I'm toast.

Win a **SHARP** MiniDisc Player

I. HOW TO ENTER

NO PURCHASE NECESSARY. Enter by printing your name, address, phone number, date of birth, and a name for the band, and mail to: SHARP & SWEET VALLEY HIGH SENIOR YEAR MINIDISC CONTEST, Random House Children's Books Marketing Department, 1540 Broadway, 19th Floor, New York, NY 10036. Entries must be received by Random House no later than July 15, 2000. LIMIT ONE ENTRY PER PERSON. Random House will not be able to return your submission, so please keep a copy for your records.

II. ELIGIBILITY

Contest is open to residents of the United States, excluding the state of Arizona, who are between the ages of 7 and 18 as of January 1, 2000. All federal, state, and local regulations apply. Void wherever prohibited or restricted by law. Employees of Random House Inc., Sharp, their parents, subsidiaries, and affiliates, and employees' immediate families and persons living in their household are not eligible to enter this contest. Random House is not responsible for lost, stolen, illegible, incomplete, postage due, or misdirected entries.

III. PRIZE

One grand prize winner and six runners-up will win a Sharp MiniDisc (approximate retail value $199.00 US).

IV. WINNER

One grand prize winner and six runners-up will be chosen on or about August 1, 2000, from all eligible entries received within the entry deadline by the Random House Children's Books Marketing Department. The contest will be judged by the Random House Children's Books Marketing Department and prizes will be awarded on the basis of creativity. The grand prize winner will receive a Sharp MiniDisc player and the winning band name may be referred to in upcoming editions of Sweet Valley High Senior Year. The six runners-up will receive Sharp MiniDisc players. Only the winners will be notified. The prizes will be awarded in the name of the winner or the winner's parent or legal guardian, if a winner is under age 18. Winners will be notified by mail on or about August 15, 2000. Taxes, if any, are the winners' sole responsibility. Each winner (or the winner's parent or legal guardian, if a winner is under age 18) will be required to execute and return affidavit of eligibility and release within 14 days of notification. A noncompliance within that time period or the return of any notification as undeliverable will result in disqualification and the selection of an alternate winner. In the event of any other noncompliance with rules and conditions, prize may be awarded to an alternate winner.

V. RESERVATIONS

By entering the contest you consent to the use of your name, likeness, and biographical data for publicity and promotional purposes on behalf of Random House and Sharp with no additional compensation or further permission (except where prohibited by law). Other entry names will NOT be used for subsequent mail solicitation. For the names of the winners, available after September 1 2000, please send a stamped, self-addressed envelope to: Random House, Sharp MiniDisc Winners, 1540 Broadway, 19th Floor, New York, NY 10036.